THE HOMECOMING

A NOVEL

by Ken McCarthy

PART ONE
The Nest

CHAPTER ONE

The lunch whistle blew, and Nick Sampson headed for the exit.

The first five hours of the workday passed with their typical, agonizing slowness. Nick could see one of the clocks from his station, and at times it seemed to stop moving. At other moments he could have sworn it was going backward. But the final three hours of the 7:00-3:30 shift would move along a little quicker.

At least for Nick.

He had been working on the production line at Kingston Bottling off and on for seven years. At 25, he had never worked anywhere else. All in all he hated it, but it was close to home and it paid pretty well.

It was a job.

Nick shouldered the push bar on the heavy steel door and walked out into a glorious spring day. He had heard somewhere that only rainy Seattle saw fewer sunny days in an average year than Pittsburgh. He didn't doubt it. And because such days were few and far between, they had to be fully enjoyed.

And I'm about to do just that, he thought.

Technically, the bottling plant wasn't in Pittsburgh proper but sat just outside its borders in the hardscrabble town of Avon. There were probably doctors and lawyers among Avon's 15,000 residents, but the vast majority of the adults (the men, anyway) either worked in the steel mills across the Monongahela River or in a business that supported those steel-making monoliths.

Nick heard that Hollywood had arrived recently in nearby Mingo Junction, Ohio to film scenes for a Vietnam War-themed movie to be called "The Deer Hunter" that would hit the big screens early the following year. From what he understood, Mingo was chosen because it was the archetype of an American mill town in 1978. He had never been to Mingo so he couldn't say if it was a good choice or not, but he thought Avon could certainly hold its own in that regard.

Dust from the mills coated everything that sat still in Avon, and the air almost always had a gritty quality to it. You cleared snow off your windshield in the winter and gray grime from it the rest of the year. It was not uncommon for an Avon resident to emerge from home in the early morning to find the message "clean me" scrawled on one of the windows of the family sedan. When he was younger, Nick himself had been guilty of that sort of finger painting on more than one occasion, and his dad, Ed, would have been surprised to know that his own Cutlass had been so decorated at his son's hands once or twice.

Well, at least when Ed Sampson was still living in Avon, that was.

And if Hollywood needed more visuals for its steel town backdrop there were always the smokestacks in the distance. Avon was built on slightly more than 1.5 square miles of land that became hillier the further east you went from the river. But regardless of your vantage point in town, you could almost always see at least the tops of the stacks perpetually billowing their gray smoke into an often-gray sky.

Nick let the door slam behind him but heard it immediately creak open again. Most of the bottling plant crew took their lunch in a little meeting room that had been hastily built into the rafters 20 feet above the work floor. With only 30 minutes for lunch, it was either bring your own food or make a mad dash to a restaurant across town. There was nothing but industrial operations in the seedy part of Avon where Kingston Bottling sat.

"Going home for lunch, Nick?"

He turned and saw that Freddy Baxter, the plant manager, had followed him out of the employee entrance. Freddy normally ate with his workers even though most of them couldn't stand him. He wasn't a bad guy but didn't handle stress well. In some work environments that might not have been a problem, but Kingston's equipment dated to the second World War and hardly ever operated the way it was supposed to, so he was always under pressure.

"Don't I always?"

Nick lived almost exactly one mile from the plant, so theoretically he could jog home, devour a sandwich and return before the back-to-work whistle sounded. And, occasionally, he did just that.

But more often than not — and especially just lately — Nick instead headed to the nest.

He was almost positive that none of his co-workers knew about his little midday diversions. Access to the nest was on the opposite side of the Kingston building from its main entrance and — at least when he first started going there — Nick always circled the building once or twice to make sure no one was watching. More recently, though, he would just quickly glance around before making a beeline to his little hidey-hole.

But was it possible Freddy had seen a change in his afternoon demeanor or performance lately and was wondering where exactly Nick was spending his break time? Or had he somehow spotted Nick coming from or going to the nest and walked over for a closer inspection? But even if he did, what would he find?

He didn't think Freddy or anyone else had a clue, but discretion was the better part of valor.

"I know I would if I were you," Freddy said. "Anything to get out of here for a few minutes."

None of the other Kingston workers lived far from the plant, but no one else lived close enough to walk.

Freddy pulled a crumpled pack of Camels out of his breast pocket and quickly fired one up. He took an extremely long pull and let out a huge cloud of blue smoke.

"Well, have a nice lunch, Nick. Tell your mom I said hi. See ya in 30," he said, then took a quick look at his wristwatch. "Make that 29."

Nick had no intention of going home and wasn't about to change his plans then, regardless of Freddy's possible suspicions. The thing was...once he got the idea of visiting the nest in his head it was almost impossible to alter course.

The bottling plant took up most of a block and was pressed up against the railroad tracks that bisected the borough. The tracks were an immutable fact of life for everyone who lived in Avon. But, unlike in other towns, there was no good or bad side of the tracks. All of Avon's residents were in the same financial boat. And that boat was listing.

Waverly Street (in reality not much more than an access alley) sat between the plant and the tracks and also led directly to Nick's mom's house. The street was in constant need of repair and was especially potholed in the area around the bottling plant where tractor-trailers assaulted the blacktop on a regular schedule, day and night, seven days a week. Pittsburghers seemingly could not get enough of the locally made, sugary beverages that Kingston pumped out.

On the far side of Waverly from the plant, a bent and twisted guard rail kept cars and pedestrians from slipping over the steep, weed-choked embankment that led first to a thin, polluted stream and ultimately to the railroad tracks themselves.

A mile further up Waverly near the Sampson's home, a path had been cut through the weeds and sumac trees over time by Nick and his older brothers and countless others who used the spot to cross to the other side of town. Growing up, Nick's parents had told him to stay off of the tracks more times than he could count. He never had a close encounter with a train himself, but there were legends galore about Avon boys who had barely escaped death after a brush with a speeding train.

Nick supposed one or two of those tales might even be true.

He headed toward home at a jog until he rounded the first bend in the road. At that point he knew without looking back that he was out of sight of the plant's employee entrance. He suspected Freddy had snubbed out his butt and headed back inside for his daily bologna sandwich and apple (occasionally a slice of pie for dessert), but he couldn't

take chances. He moved a step back toward the plant and slid behind a telephone pole.

Nick then slowly moved his head to the right until he could see the building.

All clear.

Crossing Waverly, Nick worked his way over the guard rail, down the embankment, over the stream and up onto the tracks. Every time he stood between those huge wooden ties — even as an adult — he could hear his mom's voice warning him of the imminent danger.

He knew the lunch (half) hour was quickly slipping away, so he hustled back in the direction of the building. Just as he pulled even with the third of the five truck bays on that side of the plant, the nest came into view. It was really only visible from that exact spot, and even if you were looking for it (and why would you?) it was hard to see. The nest, so dubbed by Nick's friend Gina, was in reality just a small clearing amid the shrubs and weeds. It was barely large enough for two grown adults to sit comfortably. Luckily for Nick, sharing the space had never been an issue. As he hustled toward it, he realized that Gina had only been in the nest the time she had jokingly named it, and no one else had ever visited.

"I love what you've done with the place, Nick," Gina had said on that day, which must have been about a year ago. He had cautiously told her about it a week before that, and she had been bugging him to see it since. Nick wasn't worried about Gina telling anyone about the spot or using it herself. He just didn't want her to think any less of him. "You got yourself a nice little nest here."

The name had stuck, and the nest became the basis for a constant stream of ribbing that involved Gina asking Nick for updates on his latest decorating efforts in his little hideaway.

Nick had just stepped off the tracks and started toward the stream and the nest tucked above it when he sensed movement to his right. At first, he thought Freddy had cagily waited for him to return and was about to ask Nick exactly what he was doing. But Nick quickly realized the figure was not wearing a beer-belly hugging dress shirt and tie but instead an olive-green, military-issue dress coat that once belonged to a U.S. Marine. It was torn in several places and, like its owner, was badly in need of a good washing.

Brownie.

There was no man or woman more universally recognized across Avon than Brownie, a former Marine (so the story went) who had returned from World War II to find that his wife had decided that remaining celibate while her husband was fighting in France was simply too much to ask. In fact, (so the story went) poor Brownie had actually walked in on the missus and her new beau while they were in the act. But instead of taking revenge, Brownie turned heel and headed straight to the nearest liquor store, where he had been a regular ever since.

Much like the tales of boys who barely missed getting splattered by passing trains, Nick had always assumed there was little truth to the story. The only parts that were beyond debate were that: A. Brownie always wore that Marine uniform, and B. Brownie was always drunk.

With his 30-minute lunch ticking away, Nick didn't have time to wait for Brownie to stagger off, but he didn't want the old man to see him enter the nest either. Action was needed. He reached into the front pocket of his jeans, pulled out a crumpled dollar bill and approached the old vet.

"Here ya go, Brownie. Go treat yourself. Heck, maybe it's your birthday."

Brownie could have been no taller than 5'6" standing straight up, but he was in a perpetual stoop and often seemed to be examining his battered boots even while he walked, so he appeared even shorter. He also had long, matted hair that hung in his face. Between the unclean locks and a wildly, overgrown beard, little skin above the neck was visible. But as he took the dollar from Nick's hand, Brownie turned his dirty face up, and Nick was taken aback by the two blazing blue eyes staring at him from deep in their sunken sockets. In them, Nick saw not madness but profound sadness. It occurred to him that he had probably never been that close to the old man.

"They wouldn't even tell me which way to go," Brownie whispered. Or at least that was how Nick interpreted the man's mumbled response. With that, Brownie brushed past Nick and continued down the tracks toward the heart of town, where he could find a bar on every corner that would exchange Nick's dollar for a couple of tall glasses of Schmidt's Beer.

As he watched Brownie stumble off (thinking how easy it would be for the veteran to fall, knock himself out on one of the steel rails and get run over by the next train), it occurred to Nick how many homeless vagrants there seemed to be around town lately. It was the kind of thing that was easy to miss as you went about your daily life. Those hopeless, helpless nobodies seemed to fade into — and become part of — the urban scenery, and they were only noticeable if they were in your way. Still, it seemed to Nick that their numbers had been on the rise around Avon.

The clock in Nick's head told him that he'd already lost about nine minutes of his lunch, and more time was slipping away. He shot one final look to make sure Brownie was moving on and then crossed the stream.

He climbed up into the nest.

CHAPTER TWO

Every family has stories that get repeated far more often than they deserve. These are the tales that get dragged out every Christmas morning, at every Thanksgiving dinner and often during summer picnics. They typically begin with lines like "do you remember the time John..." and go on to outline, in excruciating detail, exactly what little Johnny did in the community swimming pool the summer he turned four. Or what Mary did immediately after tasting lemons for the first time. They are rarely as funny or as entertaining as the tellers seem to believe. For the Sampsons, one such tale always began "do you remember the time that Nick locked himself in the bathroom?" *It happened early one morning in 1955, the year Nick turned two. Nick's dad, Ed, was working the graveyard shift at the mill, and his oldest brother, Nate, was off serving his country. Middle son Nevin was still sound asleep in the small bedroom the boys shared upstairs. Little Nicky, as usual, was up at the crack of dawn, playing with his toys in the living room. His mom, Ellen, was lying on the couch not far away, desperately in need of the day's first cup of coffee.*

The kitchen/dining room combo in the Sampson's first house was small, but the adjacent living room was huge and easily the home's primary selling point. And just off of the little hallway between the two rooms was a tiny washroom. It had a sink and a toilet and just enough room to stand in between them.

Ellen watched "Let's Make a Deal" reruns with one eye as she worked hard to keep the other from closing. She rarely slept well on the nights Ed was at work, which was to say she never slept well. At some point (and it was always a point of contention whether she had drifted off or just lost track of the toddler) *Nick rolled a little blue ball into the washroom and ran in after it. Ellen turned her head in that direction* (in her version of the story) *and was about to get up when the bathroom door slammed shut. A second later she heard the lock engage.*

Ellen was off the couch as if a starter's gun had been fired, and she yanked and pulled on the door while calling out for Nick to please open up. He did not. She first threatened then pleaded and finally offered all manner of reward if he would just open the door and come out. He did not. Minutes passed and Ellen had no idea what to do. By that point, Nevin had come downstairs, brown hair shooting off in all directions, rubbing sleep from his 12-year-old eyes, and asked his mom what was going on. She told him that Nick was locked in the bathroom and would not come out. Worse, (this, she did not share with Nevin) *he was not responding and, in fact, she could not hear any sounds at all coming from the bathroom.*

She eventually did the only thing that she could think of. She called the police.

Ten minutes later a squad car pulled into the driveway just ahead of a bewildered Ed Sampson, who was coming home after a long night on his feet. He asked the responding officer what was happening, but the cop seemed as unsure as Ed was himself. Ed ran ahead, yanked open the front door and found Ellen sitting on the floor trying to peer underneath the small crack at the bottom of the bathroom door. Her face was streaked with tears.

"Oh Ed, thank God you're here," she said. "Nicky's locked in there and I can't hear him!"

Ed walked over to the bathroom and did what Ellen herself had done ten thousand times already. He yanked on the door with all his might. But it wouldn't budge. Ellen rolled her eyes and silently cursed him for wasting time. Does he not think I tried to open it? she thought to herself.

The cop, whose name they would later learn was Martin, calmly walked up to the frantic Sampson parents.

"We need to take the hinges off," he said.

Nevin sprung into action and ran to grab a screwdriver from his dad's toolbox in the basement. He was back seconds later and handed the yellow-handled tool to his dad.

"I'm coming Nick," Ed said. "Sit tight."

As if he has any choice, Ellen's whirling mind thought.

The screws fell to the floor, and the hinges followed. Ed grabbed the knob and pulled. The door came off the frame with almost no resistance. He set it aside and joined the other three, who were already peering into the little bathroom.

It was empty.

For some reason (and this was a part of the story that was always emphasized, regardless of who told it) *Ed ran over and lifted the lid of the toilet. As if the boy could possibly have fit inside.* "It was the only thing I could think of," Ed always said, usually with a big grin on his face. Time had taken the edge off of the seriousness of the moment, which it often seemed to do with events that could have ended tragically but by the grace of God did not.

Finding nothing inside the toilet, he whirled around to the only other object in the room. The sink. In a microsecond, Ed Sampson's mind did the math and knew that his son was in the cabinet beneath — there was nowhere else to go — but it also insisted on telling him that little Nicky had swallowed something that he found under there. Something that should not have been in a bathroom in close proximity to a wandering toddler. "I thought he was dead," Ed would always say at that point in the tale. "I could see it in my mind's eye."

He would leave out what he had really imagined in that horrible instant: a blue-faced Nick crammed under the sink with a bright green combination of Drano and puke leaking out of his little mouth.

Ed quickly bent and opened the cabinet door. By that point, Ellen had shoved herself into the little room and was practically sitting in Ed's lap. At first, his mind told him that his vision was right. The boy was dead. Nick was curled up in the fetal position with one foot wrapped around the U-shaped pipe coming from the sink. All the blood drained from Ed's face and his breath caught.

And then Nicky shifted. Ed heard Ellen gasp and thought she was going to scream. But she had grasped the reality of the situation a split second before Ed did.

"Oh my God he's asleep," she said as the tears resumed their march down her cheeks.

"He's just sleeping."

The Sampson parents threw their arms around each other and sank to the floor. Both quietly sobbed on the other's shoulder as Nevin and officer Martin looked on.

In some tellings of the tale, the tears eventually turned to laughter.

Nick slept on.

o o o

Gina's theory — and Nick was far from buying in — was that Nick was constantly looking for the closeness and comfort that he never got from his standoffish, unaffectionate mother by burying himself in tight spaces. The incident under the bathroom sink was probably the first but certainly not the last episode that proved it, she theorized. His creation of the nest was just another example.

Nick told her (repeatedly) that she was full of shit. The nest was all about privacy, convenience and quick access, he said. After all, you just couldn't stand in the middle of the street and drink a six pack. "This isn't New Orleans," he once said.

Nick pulled aside the huge sumac branch that he always placed across the entrance of the nest and looked in. He kept expecting to walk over one day and find empty beer cans (he always took his own empties with him) and/or used condoms inside, signaling that the local teens had found the spot. But so far so good.

In the rear of the space, behind some tall weeds, he kept a thick slice of tree trunk that he had found nearby. He rolled it out into the center of the clearing and sat on it. To his left, along the rear "wall" of the nest, he had carved a makeshift shelf into the dirt. It was only visible from where he sat, and even then it was hard to see through the thick vegetation. Spring and summer were optimal nest-visiting seasons because the greenery made Nick and everything else inside nearly invisible. He had spent some lunches there in the fall too, but had never gone in the winter. Not yet, anyway.

There were three things on the shelf, and two of them Nick had placed there before reporting to work that morning. The peanut butter sandwich inside a plastic baggie (cut into squares, never triangles) and six-pack of 16-ounce Stroh's beer were Nick's normal lunch on the days he visited the nest. The third item was a photograph, also inside a baggie.

He eyed the old picture but left it where it was and grabbed the beer. It was not as cold as he would have liked, but it made no real difference. Warm beer would do the trick just as effectively as cold. He popped the top on the first one and tipped it back. Before long, his eyes watered and his throat burned (not as badly as it would have if the beer was cold though, a small victory) but he didn't stop chugging until it was empty. He took a breath, let out a huge burp and grabbed the next one. He had to take a break about halfway through beer number two. Otherwise, the process was the same. As it was with the third one.

Three beers down in about eight and a half minutes. Not bad, he thought as he looked at his watch. But Brownie and Freddy had cost Nick valuable time, and he still had to eat the sandwich. He had found that slamming so many beers on an empty stomach was just asking for trouble. But there was no way to chug peanut butter, and by the time he was done eating he had to get back to work. The beers were starting to do their thing, though, and Nick wasn't ready to call it quits. So he took number four, shoved it down the front of his jeans and underwear, and walked over to the plant.

o o o

Pepsi and Coke dominated the soda market (known as "pop" in Pittsburgh), but Kingston had carved out a nice little niche by producing a variety of unique flavors in returnable, 7-ounce glass bottles. If you attended a wedding in the 'burgh in the 70s you were sure to see cases of black grape, Hawaiian delight, creamy cherry and maybe even a bright yellow, coconut-flavored atrocity called pina colada sitting beside the mandatory kegs of Iron City beer.

The production line was a fairly straight-forward operation and required surprisingly few workers to operate. Empty bottles were put on one end of the line and full cases came off and were stacked onto (usually broken) wooden pallets at the other, with a few stops in between. At one time or another, Nick had worked every job in the plant. On the day he saw Brownie and then visited the nest he was manning a hideous contraption unofficially known as the "slitter."

After the bottles were filled, they were dropped into empty heavy-cardboard cases. Those boxes were built with the flaps folded down on the outside and held in place by small tabs. The machine's job was to "slit" those tabs, fold the freed flaps over the top of the box and then glue it shut. It was a simple concept with few moving parts.

It almost never worked right.

A couple dozen times a day a case would enter the slitter at the wrong angle or the wrong speed, and the result would be broken glass and spilled pop all over the work floor. Nick would have to smash the emergency button to stop the line and clean it up as quickly as he could. If he took too long, Freddy would appear to ask what the holdup was. Orders to fill, time is money, let's go Nick. All that happy bullshit.

Eight hours on the slitter was maddening even on a good day, but Nick had found that 48 ounces of beer (or more) really helped the second half of the day move along. Because even if the bottles were shattering all over the floor after Nick had a buzz on, his attitude didn't change much.

He didn't give a fuck.

Nick had just finished cleaning up another crash when he remembered the beer he had snuck into the building. He had placed it inside a huge carton that held the un-melted glue pellets that kept the boxes shut. None of the other work stations were visible from where he stood, but he took a quick look around anyway. The constant noise from all the machinery made it easy for someone to sneak up undetected. Seeing no one, Nick cracked the beer and finished it in one long pull. He smashed the empty under his heel, threw it into a nearby garbage can and covered it with some other debris. A minute later he heard a voice.

"Hey Sampson, where's Delilah?"

Nick turned and saw Bill Morton walking his way. Bill had seniority among the plant's workers, and so he also had perhaps the softest job. The forklifts would place pallets loaded with cases of empty bottles near Bill's station at the head of the production line. His job was simply to get the cases onto the rollers to start the pop-making process. It was as simple as simple could be, and Nick often thought it would surely drive him mad if he had to do it day after day.

Of course, running the slitter didn't exactly require a PhD.

Nick knew that Bill was basically a good guy and meant no harm by the Delilah crack. But he had heard that same line so many times throughout his life that he still became annoyed. Nick started wearing his hair long as a teenager, but that only added fuel to the Samson and Delilah fire. It didn't seem to matter when he explained to his tormentors that Samson of Biblical fame didn't even spell his name the same way Nick did.

Nevertheless, Nick had worn his hair in a Marine-style buzzcut for the past eight years. "I just put the last of the cherry on, and then we're switching over to orange," Bill said. The plant typically produced two or three different flavors on any given day. Morton tipped his chin toward the slitter. "How's your hunk of junk today?"

"The usual. An unmitigated disaster."

"Lot of that going around," Bill said. He bent and picked up a stray piece of glass from the cement floor then tossed it into a nearby can. "Hey, I haven't heard anything for a while on your mom. How's she been?"

Nick's normal happy-go-lucky demeanor evaporated, and Bill wondered if he might have crossed some line he didn't know existed. He quickly backtracked.

"I don't mean to pry, Nick. Sorry. Just making conversation."

"It's fine. She's ok I guess." Nick gave him a weak smile then turned and headed over to dump more glue pellets into the slitter. Bill quickly headed back the way he came.

A change in flavor meant the production line workers would get about a 10-minute break as the end of the cherry was flushed from the system and the orange took its place. It was a chance to grab a quick smoke and/or take a piss. With 64 ounces of beer in his system, Nick was more concerned with the latter. He walked over to the little bathroom in the rear of the building but saw that three others were already waiting. The restroom accommodated only one person at a time. It was a ridiculous setup, and the employees had complained to Freddy about it for years. As plant manager, Freddy used the second-floor facilities that were reserved for management and office staff, so the complaints fell on deaf ears.

"Stupid fuck," Nick mumbled to himself as he headed back to his station. By the time he got there, the situation with his bladder was becoming more urgent, and Nick started considering alternatives. There was an open sewer system that ran throughout the plant to catch spilled soda and to make hosing the floor at the end of each shift easier. *Any port in a storm*, Nick thought, and unzipped his fly. He grabbed a nearby broom so that it would look to anyone who might be watching like he was just sweeping. Then he let his bladder loose.

Nick was finding that urinating in strange places was becoming somewhat of a regular occurrence.

It was one of the unspoken side effects of doing a lot of drinking.

o   o   o

Nick was first out the door when the whistle blew at 3:30. He needed a drink. No matter what time of day he had his first beer, he noticed that cutting off the alcohol was...well it wasn't exactly painful, but it was certainly uncomfortable. As his beer-buzz wore off, he often felt like he had bugs crawling just beneath the surface of his skin. So far, the only two effective remedies he had found were sleep or more beer.

He strolled up Waverly Street at a casual pace to give his co-workers time to get to their cars and head home. No one ever dawdled at quitting time so he wouldn't have to wait long. To his left was the railroad and to his right were a string of row houses, duplexes and a few small, single-family homes. Most had seen better days and were in dire need of fresh paint and a good grass cutting. Many of the yards were fenced in, and a few of those held dogs that always seemed pissed off. Nick was used to being barked at almost the entire time he walked to and from work each day.

From an open window on one of the row houses, Nick could hear Harry Chapin singing his soulful, heart-breaking ballad about fathers and sons. The song wasn't getting as much airtime as it did when it was first released a couple of years back, but Nick thought it was a rare week when he didn't catch "Cat's in the Cradle" on the radio at least once. Or maybe he was just especially sensitive to the lyrics, so it only seemed to follow wherever he went. *"When you comin' home dad? I don't know when..."*

After a few minutes he turned around and headed back the other way and was not surprised to see the employee parking lot was completely deserted. He stepped over the guardrail and ducked into the nest. He reached into some weeds and pulled out the paper bag that he had brought his lunch in that morning. Nick threw the three empties into it and was about to add the two full beers when he noticed that crawling sensation along his arms and the back of his neck again. At least that's where it seemed to be coming from. It was really a whole-body awfulness, and it was tough to pinpoint the area of origin.

"But I know how to fix it," he said to no one in particular.

He grabbed one of the beers (even warmer now, having sat in the sun all day) opened it and took a long pull. He was about to finish it when he noticed the picture in the baggie laying on his little shelf. He put the half-full beer on the ground and picked up the photo.

It was fraying along the edges and yellowing from age, but even through the plastic he could make out the people in the photo clearly. Or maybe it only seemed that way. He had looked at the picture so many times that he knew it like the back of his hand.

In the photo, a smiling Ed Sampson was standing on a beach flanked on each side by his older two sons. Eleven-year-old Nick stood directly in front of his dad, and Ed had a hand on each of Nick's sun-browned shoulders.

Nick didn't know for certain, but he believed it was the last photo ever taken of the four Sampson men together.

CHAPTER THREE

Even before so much went wrong, the Sampsons were never going to be confused with the Andersons from "Father Knows Best." Part of the problem was that it was hard to build a typical American family when a couple's three children were born over a span of two full decades. It just wasn't something you saw every day. Whenever someone found out that Nick and Nate were brothers — and that Nate wasn't actually Nick's very young father — there were certain assumptions that followed. Many people automatically believed that one of the boys were unplanned. Others wondered quietly if the parents had separated for a period, only to reunite and reproduce again years later. Some even suspected that Nick was fathered by someone other than Ed, who was pushing 45 when Nick was born.

But none of that was true.

The reality was much simpler. Ed and Ellen had never "planned" for any of the three boys but neither did they ever take any action ("the pill" was just being developed the year Nick was born) to prevent a pregnancy, and birth control was never considered. The fact was that Ellen, who miscarried early in a pregnancy in 1938, had only gotten pregnant four times, and they just so happened to span 20 years.

But maybe Ed and Ellen at one point envisioned having something that at least resembled an apple pie-eating, July 4 sparkler-waving, all-American family. Nick thought it was the only plausible explanation for why they had given all three boys names that began with the letter N. They were trying to be cute and trendy. Both parents where coy when asked about it over the years, but there was no way it was a coincidence. There were no Nicks or Nates on either side of the family tree. And Nevin? Nevin? Where the hell did that come from?

No, they clearly did it on purpose. But why? Nick had asked himself (and his parents) that question countless times. And, if they were going down that path, why wouldn't Ed and Ellen choose three names that began with E? Or a letter that lent itself to a bunch of solid names. K, for instance, would have allowed for Kevin, Ken, Keith and even Kelly. But Nevin? Jesus.

o o o

The Sampson house resembled many in Avon,
which was to say it was a small structure on a
small lot with barely enough room to shine a
flashlight beam between it and the homes on
either side. Its one distinguishing characteristic
was that it was painted an odd salmon color for
no apparent reason. Ellen Sampson sold the
larger house where Nick had holed up in the
downstairs bathroom shortly after Ed left town.

She simply couldn't afford the mortgage on her
meager income, which primarily consisted of
public assistance and a small amount of "rent"
from Nick. The "new" house was smaller, older
and had no real yard in the front.

Nick bounded up the two steps onto the sagging
wooden porch and looked back over his shoulder
as a train thundered into view on the other side of
Waverly. That was one similarity between the
two homes: both were within spitting distance of
the railroad tracks.

Inside, a short, paneled hallway led to a large,
yellow kitchen at the rear of the house. But Nick
took a quick right into the only other room on the

first floor. His mom was sitting on an old brown sofa watching the new RCA television in the corner. For more than a dozen years, the sofa had also served as her bed. She had not slept on the old queen mattress upstairs since Ed took off.

Ellen had just turned up the volume on the TV to keep the passing train from drowning out her game show but turned it back down as Nick walked in.

"Hey mom." He kicked his work boots off and hung his jacket on a hook just outside the living room. The hallway was narrow enough that Nick could easily touch both walls at the same time. "Did you make it to the pharmacy?"

She bent and set her drink on the scarred coffee table in front of the couch. It was always Pepsi for Ellen and never the Kingston knockoff (Rite Cola), even though Nick could get as much of it as he wanted for free. "No, I was hoping you'd run over," she said. "You could grab something for dinner while you're out if you want."

Nick grunted. It wasn't that he didn't want to walk to the Revco Pharmacy or that he was worried about her missing a dose of her meds (he wasn't, and in fact he was concerned about her growing dependence on them) but he was hoping she would have gone out, if only for a short walk. She hardly ever left the house anymore.

At 65, Ellen Sampson was fed up with life and all its pain and was only looking forward to the end. This wasn't something Nick guessed at or inferred from her actions. It was something she told him all time. "I just want to be done, Nicky. I'm ready to go join my boys."

"Please don't say that mom," he would always counter, although a cowardly part of himself that he despised knew his life would be easier if she was gone.

He wondered if she even knew how hurtful her reasoning was to him. *"What about me,*

Mom? Don't you want to stick around for the son who's still here?"

It was getting harder by the day for Nick to remember the woman and mother she had been before everything fell apart. He could conjure up a few random images, including one of a much younger Ellen sitting on the beach in the vacation town of Pocataw, Pennsylvania, where that old photo of the four Sampson men was shot. Or another in which she was putting little blue candles on his birthday cake the year he turned 9. But beyond that there wasn't much. That younger, happier version of his mom was slipping into the void.

And, to be honest, Nick had a hard time blaming her. Losing two sons and a husband was more than most women could handle.

Three strikes and Ellen Sampson was out.

o o o

In many ways, the world that Nick had known for his first 12 years on the planet came to an end on April 12, 1965. That afternoon, a black sedan pulled up in front of the Sampson house, and two Marines wearing dress blues approached the door.

Nick and his parents were in the living room watching television when the soldiers stepped out of the car. Because of where he was sitting, Nick was the first to see them approach. He had no idea what they could possibly want, but something deep inside told him the news was bad. Very bad.

"Dad," was all he managed to say as he watched the men approach through the room's large, picture window.

Ed heard something off in Nick's tone and quickly looked up. He watched the color drain from his son's face and — following his gaze — saw the Marines step up onto the porch.

"No," he whispered.

Ellen, sitting in the far corner, had no idea what Nick and Ed were looking at, but alarm bells were ringing inside her head. She got to Ed's side just as the one of the soldiers knocked on the old wooden door. How his mom immediately understood why the Marines were there was never clear to Nick, even years later.

But she knew.

Ellen pressed both hands to her mouth and shrieked. It was an inhuman sound that Nick had never heard before and would never forget. It still occasionally haunted his dreams. Ed quickly grabbed for his wife, but she was already sprinting to the front door, wailing even louder. She threw the door open and screamed at the two Marines, who seemed unflappable despite the situation unfolding before them. Part of

Ed's mind crazily wondered how many times they must have witnessed similar scenes.

"Don't say it!" she bellowed at them. "Don't you dare!"

Ed thought for a moment that Ellen was going to assault the Marines, anything to stop them from doing what they came to the house to do. He grabbed her and spun her toward him.

"Ellen stop," he said more forcefully than he intended. "Look." He turned her toward Nick, who was standing still as a statue, his face white as a sheet.

Seeing the shock on Nick's face had the same effect as a slap to her own, and Ellen regained at least a modicum of composure. She took a deep breath and turned to face the Marines. The taller of the two stepped forward. "Are you mister and missus Sampson?" he asked. Ed nodded as Ellen let out a sob. "The Commandant of United States Marines Corp has asked me to convey his deep regrets that your son Nathan was killed in action outside the city of Da Nang in South Vietnam. The Commandant sends his deepest sympathy to you and your family for this tragic loss."

There was more to the prepared speech, but none of the Sampsons heard it. Ed and Nick were by then kneeling beside Ellen, who had collapsed onto the hallway floor.

The grandfather clock in the living room continued to tick off the seconds, indifferent.

o o o

Nate Sampson enlisted in the Marines not long after his high school graduation and remained in the Corps until his death. Both of his parents were caught off guard when he first told them of his plans. Nate had never been especially patriotic and had talked instead about possibly enrolling in junior college in the fall.

"It's the right thing to do," he told his parents the evening after he took the oath. He didn't tell them ahead of time because he didn't want them trying to talk him out of it.

The average age of a soldier in Vietnam was 19, but Nate was 32 when he and 5,000 other Marines landed at Da Nang in March of 1965 as part of the first wave of American involvement in the war. He had advanced to the rank of Gunnery Sergeant not long before he shipped out. Nate had only been in country about a month when he was killed in a skirmish near the U.S. airbase that the 9th Marine Expeditionary Brigade had been sent to South Vietnam to protect.

o o o

The year following the news of Nate's death had a dream-like quality for Nick. He continued with the activities that had comprised the bulk of his life before Nate died — junior high school, baseball in the spring, football in the fall — but most of the time he felt like a ghost hovering just outside his body, watching someone else live his life. Ed and Ellen might have taken him to a psychologist to work through the grief if they had noticed the changes in their youngest son. But they were locked in their own solitary cells of despair and barely took notice of the boy, even when Nick was in the same room.

The three of them drifted through the 12 months that followed the visit from the Marines with little interaction and each of them, separately, focused solely on getting through the day before them. Putting one foot in front of the other. The house often felt like a morgue, and talk was at a minimum. Behind closed doors, Ed and Ellen watched helplessly as the marriage they had bult over more than three decades slowly slipped through their fingers like sand.

So when the one-year anniversary of Nathan's death rolled around on a Tuesday in April 1966, Ellen was little surprised to find Nick home alone when she returned from a trip to the supermarket. Ed Sampson was gone.

o o o

While his parents and younger brother rattled around their Avon home that year, Nevin

Sampson kept his distance. Like Nate, he moved out of the house as soon as he turned 18, but unlike his older brother, Nevin chose college over the military. He walked away from Washington and Jefferson College four years later with a B.A. of Fine Arts degree in photography. Because he was born in 1943, Nevin was slightly too old to qualify for the military draft lottery that was held late in 1969, but he ultimately went to Southeast Asia anyway.

When he got there, he was carrying a camera instead of a rifle. He was looking for Nate's ghost.

CHAPTER FOUR

The guy in the black hoodie was back.

Gina saw him walk into the store during the final hour of her shift. She had noticed the same guy in the store two days before. He was memorable among the hundreds of Revco customers she saw each day because of the hoodie, which he kept tightly cinched over his head, and because of the oversized dark sunglasses he wore, even inside the brightly-lit store. She had a feeling he was trying to blend in and look inconspicuous, but Gina Marino thought he was doing a pretty shitty job of it.

He looked like a guy with shoplifting on his mind.

Gina had to remain at the cash register to check out customers, so she couldn't keep too close an eye on him as he wandered through the drugstore. The guy walked down the toothpaste/deodorants aisle, but Gina lost track of him when he moved toward the back of the store. She was about to try to get the attention of Terry, the stock boy, when Hoodie emerged from the aisle with the new paperbacks and magazines

(Lose 15 pounds in a week!) a minute later and headed right toward her. It looked like his hands were empty.

"Good afternoon," Gina greeted him. "Find everything ok?"

Seeing him up close only reinforced Gina's initial feeling about the guy. Something wasn't quite right. He set a pack of AA batteries on the counter. "Yeah, just these."

"Great, that'll be 99 cents," she said as she hit the buttons on the cash register.

The man reached into the right pocket of the hoodie and pulled out a $50. He offered it to her.

"You have anything smaller?" she asked. "We don't keep much change up front in the registers."

That wasn't exactly true, but her sense that something was wrong had only intensified since he pulled out the large bill. She was worried about the guy grabbing a handful of cash and taking off. It had happened before.

"Sorry," he said and shrugged.

Gina reluctantly took the $50 and opened her cash drawer. As she was counting out the change, Hoodie reacted to something happening outside the store's large, front window.

"Oh Jesus, did you see that?" he asked. "That delivery truck just backed into that blue car. I think he's just gonna leave!"

Gina craned her neck but didn't have a good view of the parking lot from her vantage point on the other side of the counter. She leaned out as far as she could but couldn't see anything amiss outside. "It's a crazy world," she said.

Gina wanted nothing more than to complete the transaction and get the guy out of the store, and quickly. She turned back and saw Hoodie reaching into the front of his jeans. There was a little line of customers forming behind him.

"Hey, I do have a $5 after all," he said. "Here ya go. Sorry about that. Can I have the $50 back. I'll need that for the bar tonight." He gave her a sly smile and looked her up and down. "You ever hang out at the Red Door?"

"Um, no. It's a pretty bad scene over there." She handed the large bill back and took the smaller one.

"Suit yourself."

Gina gave him the receipt and the change for the $5. Then she handed him a little paper bag with the batteries inside. "Have a good one," he said.

Seeing the guy walking away from the register did not make Gina feel any better. In fact, she thought something was still very wrong, but she couldn't put her finger on what it was.

Until he was about halfway to the front door. Then it clicked.

"Hey, stop!" she yelled. "Get back here!"

In a flash, Gina leapt over the counter and headed straight for Hoodie, who was at that point running for the door. Customers looked on in shock, afraid to move.

"Gary, get him!" she yelled at the store's security guard. The most excitement Gary Watson saw in an ordinary day was helping some of Avon's senior citizens get their purchases out to their cars. He sat in his chair near the door unmoving, unsure of what was happening as Gina tore across the front of the store.

Just as Hoodie grabbed the door handle, Gina dove for his legs. Anyone watching might have been reminded of Pittsburgh Steeler linebacker Jack Lambert going after Earl Campbell at the goal line. She hit him mid-thigh and held on tight. "Give it back you bastard!" she yelled.

Hoodie seemed equal parts surprised and pissed off. He tried valiantly to shake her from his legs while at the same time pulling on the front door. But Gina wouldn't budge.

"Get off of me you crazy bitch! What's wrong with you?"

"Gary, get the cops over here!"

Gary had gotten to his feet but stood still, unsure what he was supposed to do. But when Hoodie began raining punches down on the back of Gina's head, he quickly moved in and grabbed the guy's arms. Gary was 60 and retired, but he stood 6'3" and had spent his career working on the railroads ("all the live-long day," he would often tell people). When he wrapped his arms around Hoodie the battle was effectively over.

"Let's all go in the back and wait for the police," he said to a panting, squirming Hoodie. "We'll get this all straightened out in no time."

As Gina gained her feet and Gary led Hoodie to the small lunch room in the back, a small crowd that had been watching the scene unfold from outside the store tentatively walked inside. One of them was Nick Sampson.

"So, how's it going?" he asked Gina, suppressing a little smile. She was brushing herself off, and he noticed an ugly cut on the palm of her left hand.

"Oh just peachy," Gina said. "Another night in paradise."

o o o

"So explain to me how this scam works again," Nick said to Gina as they walked out of the store an hour later. He had been on his way into the store to pick up his mom's prescription (and a Reese's Cup for himself) and got there just in time to see Gary wrap his meaty paws around the guy in the black hoodie. "You know I'm a little slow on the uptake. But I might want to try it myself sometime." "I wouldn't be surprised," she said. They turned down Church Street and walked past St. Matthias. The old Catholic church and the surrounding grounds were quiet, and Nick thought to himself that there was nothing quite as eerie as an empty church at night.

Spring had definitely arrived in Western Pennsylvania, but the night air still had a little bite to it.

"He gave me the $50 then distracted me with some bullshit story about a hit-and-run outside while I gave him the change," Gina explained. "Then he gives me a $5 and asks for the $50 back. So I gave him change for both the $50 and the $5 and he walks away with a quick $48 profit."

"You mean $49, right," Nick said. He was trying to work the transaction out in his head as she explained it, but math was never his strong suit. The slitter at Kingston required no calculations from its operator.

"No, because he basically paid for the batteries twice."

"Ok, I got it."

"I doubt it," she said and rapped him on the shoulder.

Gina lived with her parents two streets over from the Sampsons. Both families had been Avon residents from time immemorial. Gina's dad, Frank, and Nick's dad, Ed, both grew up in Avon during World War 1, and neither had ever lived anywhere else (except, of course, Ed now resided God-knew-where). But while Ed Sampson was grinding out a living in the steel mills, Frank Marino built a career as an accountant. Mr. Marino's job was — for reasons that were never clear to Nick — a sore spot for Ed. When Nick and Gina first met, Ed told his youngest son he had no respect for a man who wore a tie to work and sat behind a desk all day.

"Take a look at his hands sometime, Nicky," Ed Sampson had said on more than one occasion. "You can tell a lot about a man by the number of callouses on his hands."

Even at a young age, Nick thought it would be pretty cool to have a job that didn't send you home physically exhausted every night. But he kept those thoughts to himself.

Nick and Gina approached the corner of Church and McClure. The Marino house was halfway down the block on the right. No one else was around, and the neighborhood was quiet.

"Here's the spot where we officially met," Nick said as they turned and started down the street. "Right here." It wasn't something he pointed out every time they walked down the street, but he did it often enough to annoy Gina.

"Yes," she sighed. "I am aware."

o o o

Nick and Gina were both in the fifth grade, though they attended different classrooms at Dickson Elementary. There were three fifth-grade classes, and the students remained in the same room with the same teacher for all their courses throughout the day. Not until the kids went to the new junior high school up on the hill in seventh grade did they move from room to room each period for different subjects.

Dickson was one of three elementary schools in Avon, and the kids for the most part walked to and from the buildings. Because Nick and Gina lived on the same side of town, they knew each other, but only in the most literal of ways. They certainly did not hang in the same social circle. Most 10-year-olds stuck strictly within their own gender when it came to making friends, but that was not what kept Nick and Gina apart.

Instead, it was because they were both loners who mainly kept to themselves

(separately) with few close friends. That could have been partly due to the fact that both were basically only-children who did not have the advantage of learning socialinteraction skills with other kids at home. Gina had no siblings, and Nick's brothers were 10 and 20 years older than him and lived elsewhere anyway.

One blustery day in March of that year, Nick was walking home and thinking of nothing but pulling out his baseball card collection when he got there. He had to figure out exactly which cards he needed to complete the Topps set. Gina was walking slightly ahead and on the opposite side of Church Street. She would turn onto McClure (he knew this because he had seen her do it so many times) and he would continue on Church for two more blocks before turning onto Center. As he approached McClure, he looked across the street and saw Gina standing still and staring into the distance. He couldn't tell what she was looking at. Nick probably would have paid her no more mind (although he was kind of curious about what was holding her *attention) and kept moving, but as he watched, Gina dropped all her books to the ground. And, even more strange, she didn't even seem to notice. She just went on staring down the street.*

Nick stopped and watched. Gina still wasn't moving.

More curious than concerned, Nick waited for a gap in the traffic and ran across the street. He approached Gina slowly while trying to figure out what she was looking at. "Hey, is everything..." He stopped cold. Gina's face was devoid of all color and her eyes were wide open, unblinking. Her mouth was moving but only garbled sounds were coming out.

"Hey, you ok?" Nick would have never admitted it but he was scared, and more than just a little. He was about to put his hand on her arm when she started gently rocking, from the balls of her feet to her heels and then back. Back and forth, back and forth. Nick had seen enough. He wasn't positive which house was hers, but he thought it was one of two about halfway down the block. He left Gina and bolted down McClure. As he approached the first that he thought might be Gina's home (brick with a light blue awning), a woman walked out the front door onto the porch. It was almost as if she was expecting him.

"Where's Gina?" she asked.

"Um, she's standing down on the corner ma'am. She's just standing there. She's not moving. I think something is wrong."

Without a word, Mrs. Marino brushed past Nick and ran up the block. Nick wasn't sure what to do, so he stayed put and watched as she approached Gina at the end of the street. Gina's mom dropped down in front of the girl and put a hand on each of her arms. She stayed that way for a whole minute. At that point, it looked like Gina was coming around although it was hard to tell from where Nick was standing. He thought he could hear her talking to her mother. She seemed to be ok.

Part of Nick wanted to just take off and go home (using an alternate route so he could avoid the Marinos), but the more curious part of him that wanted to stick around ultimately won out. It wasn't that he was being "nebby" (his mom's word for nosy) or that he wanted a thank you for his role in the incident, whatever it was.

He was just worried about Gina.

Eventually Gina's mom put her arm around the girl's shoulders and walked her slowly down the block. As *they approached Nick, Gina seemed to blush and looked away. They stopped in front of Nick.*

"You're a Sampson, right?" Mrs. Marino asked.

He nodded. "Yeah, I'm Nick."

"Well thank you Nick. You were a big help today."

Like Gina, Nick was examining the ground around his shoes. He didn't know what to say. "No problem," he said.

Mrs. Marino squeezed his arm and led her daughter up the steps to the porch and then inside. Gina never looked back.

o o o

"And I got no thank you, no nothing," Nick said. "At least not from you."

"A thousand pardons, your wonderfulness," she said. "How could I be so rude?" She rapped him on the shoulder again, this time with a little more force. "So how did you find out what really happened?" Gina asked. "Who told you about my... situation?" They were walking again and almost to the small yard in front of Gina's house. He noticed (for the millionth time) that Gina herself never used the word epilepsy. Never.

"My mom told me when I got home. But I don't know how she knew."

Gina laughed and started up the walk toward her house. Before she got to the steps, she turned back to Nick.

"There is no communication system in the world as effective as the Avon-mothers grapevine, Nick. None."

CHAPTER FIVE

While Gina quietly dealt with epilepsy, Nick had issues of his own. In addition to the drinking, which was becoming alarming (to Gina, anyway), he was also dealing with anxiety and it's horrifying big brother, panic attacks. Nick, though, didn't have a name for those terrifying feelings. They were a relatively new development in his life and something he talked about to no one. Other than his mother and Gina, there really *was* no one to talk to. He certainly wasn't going to add to his mom's woes, and he just wasn't ready yet to tell Gina. Once or twice he thought about bringing it up to her but stopped short. Just as he initially kept the existence of the nest from her, he was simply worried about what she would think of him.

Most of the time the anxious feelings were mild anyway. No big deal. Just a little too much stress in his life, he figured. Except on the days when he had a lot of coffee, it was often just a sense of something being not quite right inside his body. Like there was a little too much juice in his nerve endings and he couldn't quite settle down. His mind would latch onto some small thing-a strange sensation in belly for instance- and wouldn't let go. He could get himself worked up (on the inside) over almost anything and was often convinced he was dying. Luckily, the feeling usually faded as quickly as it popped up.

But other times, including days when he was overcaffeinated,...well Nick was growing increasingly alarmed about the frequency and intensity of those attacks. And, the worst part was, his own mind was at the root of the problem. How did you battle something that started within your own head with virtually no cause and little warning? It was terrifying. He really wanted to talk to someone about it because he thought that just hearing it described out loud, with his own ears, would lessen the panic's crippling power over him. Or something. He decided that he would talk to Gina about it the next time he saw her.

But for now, Nick would still have to face the nights on his own. For some reason, the attacks seemed to hit more often after the sun had gone down. It made no sense, but, well, there you had it. No one in Pittsburgh was happier that those short, bleak winter days were in the rear-view mirror than Nick Sampson. Spring meant days of longer sunlight, and thus less time in darkness. Nick sometimes envisioned his panic as a vampire, hiding in its dusty coffin throughout the day, quietly biding its time until nightfall. And once the sun fell behind those rolling Western Pennsylvania hills...all bets were off.

And just recently there had been a new (dreadful) twist added into the mix. Nick was having some bad nightmares, and they in turn were setting the panic train in motion. He would usually go to bed around 11 o'clock and hardly ever had trouble falling asleep. But he would snap awake at 1:30 or 2:00 a.m. with his heart racing, unable to shake off the clinging cobwebs of the dream.

Just two nights earlier he had suffered through a particularly disturbing nightmare. He had finished Stephen King's novel *The Shining* the week before, and it was likely on his mind as he drifted off.

Because in the dream...

Nick was alone in the ballroom of a huge, old hotel. It was night and the room was dark. The only illumination came from weak moonlight filtering through the large, bay windows. He walked over to the nearest wall and flipped the light switch, but nothing happened. Up down. Up down. Nothing. In the dream, Nick began to feel uneasy.

Because something was in the room with him. He couldn't see it or hear it, but he knew beyond a shadow of a doubt that it was there. Waiting. Watching him. He fought a growing sense of panic and stood as still as one of the marble statues in the courtyard outside. He listened. One minute passed. Two.

Nick started walking slowly toward the exit and the courtyard beyond. He knew that if he ran (IT) the thing would emerge from its hiding place. It would pounce.

He reached the patio and then walked out onto an expansive, manicured lawn. He breathed a sigh of relief. Nothing had followed him outside. Nick looked up into an endless black sky. There was not a cloud in sight, but no stars were shining. Only the moon looked back. It provided no comfort though. In fact, it looked to Nick as if a face on its bright white surface was scowling at him.

Inexplicably, (as movements in dreams often were, especially nightmares) Nick was compelled to go back inside. There was some unnamed task he knew he must perform. He had no choice. He crossed the lawn and courtyard and opened the door. Again, nothing but darkness waited inside. Nick quickly crossed the room and again threw up the light switch. This time, the antique globes overhead flashed on before immediately going off again. In that moment of illumination Nick thought he saw a figure standing at the other end of the room. And just as darkness claimed the space again, he heard a voice that seemed to come from everywhere and nowhere at the same time.

"I haunt," it whispered.

Nick tore from the ballroom, but rather than face the glaring moon outside he headed deeper into the hotel. He ran down a dark corridor with guest rooms lining both sides. All of the doors were open, but none of the rooms were occupied. Except one. As he ran past that room, Nick could see a tall figure standing just inside the doorway. He paused. It looked like it was wearing a top hat. No other features were visible. It did not move or speak.

Nick ran on down the seemingly-endless hallway.

Eventually he reached a T-junction and turned left into another deserted space. It looked like a dining room. *Countless large, round tables were set, as if for dinner. Nick quickly crossed it, weaving through the tables and chairs, wanting nothing but to get out of the old building as fast as he could. He would rather face the haunted moon again than whatever it was he saw in that guest room. The exit on the far side of the large space led to a stone path that first traversed open, manicured grounds but quickly moved into dense forest.*

Trees crowded in on both sides, and Nick ran. The moon above was no friend but it provided enough light for Nick to follow the large half-buried stones that comprised the path beneath his feet. They appeared unnaturally white in the moonlight.

They look like the tops of headstones, *Nick thought crazily.*

He ran on.

Eventually, he came to a small meadow. And, beyond that, a pond. Nick sprinted to the edge of the dark water and tried to catch his breath. He bent over with his hands on his knees, eyes on the ground around his feet. A minute passed and he felt compelled to look up. Don't do it! he told himself. Do not look over there! But he was powerless to stop.

On the far side of the pond stood a tall, thin figure. It wore a top hat that Nick knew beyond any doubt was as black as the night sky above.

It opened its hideous mouth and uttered just one word, the whispery voice carrying across the still water.

"Come," it said.

"No!"

Nick sat bolt upright in bed. He was sweating and his heart was hammering. He took a few deep breaths and tried to get his racing pulse under control. Nick kept trying to divert his mind to anything other than the image of that ghastly figure across the pond. But the more he tried the harder it became. Once, on a day after a similar attack, it occurred to him that it was like telling yourself NOT to think about a pink zebra.

He sat as still as he could and fought the urge to get up and run from the room. He had done that before and knew from experience that it would only exacerbate the problem. Giving into the panic only led his mind to believe that there *was* actually something to panic about. No, he would not do that again. Staying calm and remaining in bed was the key to regaining control. He had succeeded before. He could do it again, he told himself.

But it was so hard. One minute he would feel like he was calming and the next he would start spiraling toward the panic again. In his mind, he pictured his emotions as a rollercoaster at Pittsburgh's Kennywood Park. Up and down. Down and up. And over what? A silly image of a vague monster conjured up by his stressed-out, restless mind. Did he really think it was it going to walk out of the nightmare and materialize there in his bedroom?

In the light of day such thoughts were easily dismissed as ridiculous, but in the middle of the night anything seemed possible. Anything at all.

o o o

By 1978, Nick had lived almost as long with his dad out of his life (12 years) than in it (13 years). He had not laid eyes on Ed Sampson since that day in the spring of 1966 when he left his family and Avon behind for good. Nick had no idea if his dad was dead or alive. He didn't know if Ed lived right around the corner or in Hawaii. Maybe he moved to Vietnam to be closer to his two lost sons.

For the first few months after his father left, many of the men Nick spotted around town seemed to resemble his dad, at least from a distance. Once, Nick and his mom were at Elko's garage picking up the Cutlass after getting some work done on it (Ed left on foot, and Ellen kept the old car for a couple of years after) when Nick saw a man he was sure was his dad walking down the street.

Nick was looking out of the shop's plate glass window, casually watching the foot traffic on Salem Street while his mom talked to old Brian Elko about the repair work. He was thinking of little other than getting home and eating before baseball practice later that day, when his breath caught. His eyes grew wide, and his mouth formed an elongated O.

The guy was the same height and age as Ed Sampson and wore dirty green coveralls just like Ed (and 99% of the mill workers in town) did. He even had the same quick stride. Nick was positive it was him.

"Mom," he said, never taking his eyes off the guy strolling down the street toward the Village Dairy.

Ellen was talking to Mr. Elko about looming brake problems with the car and didn't hear him.

He was ready to call her again but realized that she was in the middle of a conversation. Nick quickly pivoted back to the window and saw the man was standing at the intersection at Hazel Street and was waiting to cross. Without another thought, Nick bolted out the front door and headed in his direction. He could not let his dad get away. As he ran, he thought about what he was going to say. A million ideas ran through his mind but none of them seemed quite right. The important thing was just to make contact. They could work the rest out later, he told himself.

Nick reached the corner just as the guy was preparing to cross the street. He seemed to notice Nick at his side just as Nick tentatively put his hand out to touch his arm. As the stranger turned and looked down to face him, Nick's mind filled in Ed's facial features. It was him.

"Dad," Nick squeaked, barely a whisper.

"'Are you lost, son?" the man asked.

The use of the word "son" only further confused Nick's overheated brain. He did a double-take and for the first time took a real look at the guy. The mustache was the *most obvious giveaway because Nick had never known his dad to wear one. Any extra hair was a no-no in the mill. But, even beyond that, the similarities were minimal. How could he have been so dumb?*

He started trying to think of something to say, but the guy was already marching across the street, the brief episode seemingly forgotten.

Confused, embarrassed and dejected, Nick walked back to the garage. He saw that Mr. Elko had pulled the Cutlass out of the service bay and into the front lot. His mom was standing there watching him approach. She held her purse firmly in front of her body with both hands. Nick had no idea if she had seen any of the exchange with the man on the corner. He tried to read her face but could not.

"I thought..." but he didn't even have to finish.

"I know what you thought, Nick," his mom said. "But forget about him. He's gone." She turned and headed toward the driver's side of the car, and Nick stood still. He could barely hear the rest of what she said, and it didn't matter anyway. But he was pretty sure her last words as she climbed into the car were "and good riddance."

CHAPTER SIX

"Gina, wait"

Nick stood on the sidewalk in front of the Marino's house. The neighborhood streets were deserted that late on a work night. The house itself looked locked up tight for the night too. Mr. Marino was no doubt already in bed with eight hours of balance sheets and debits and credits waiting for him the next day. Gina's mother had never worked — at least as far as Nick knew — and he wasn't sure how she spent her days. As he stood there, it occurred to Nick that he really didn't know much at all about either of Gina's parents. Was that strange? Should he have known more personal details about his best friend's parents? Nick wasn't sure.

Gina stopped with her hand on the doorknob. She turned back to Nick.

"Yes?"

Nick was deep in thought wondering if Mrs. Marino just sat around the house all day watching sitcom reruns and gameshows (like his mom) waiting for her husband to return from work (unlike his mom) and didn't hear Gina reply. What *did* she do all day?

"What Nick?"

"Oh sorry. Just daydreaming. Or evening dreaming, I guess. Anyway, I was going to ask if you wanted to go get a drink. You don't work until noon again tomorrow, right? We could just walk up to the Triangle."

The idea of a tall, cold draft beer actually sounded pretty good to Gina. Especially after her encounter at the drug store with Hoodie (real name Ben Burkman, age 28) and then the cops afterward. Like Nick, they at first couldn't seem to grasp the math of what Burkman had almost pulled off.

"How about the Dairy Delite instead?" The beer definitely sounded better than a cone, but Gina had become increasingly concerned about Nick's drinking and did not want to contribute to it. He had been drinking since the year they turned 18 — so had she, to be honest — but in the past year it had escalated rapidly both in terms of frequency and sheer volume. Even setting aside the incident last week when he got the flat tire (and God that was scary), there were warning bells ringing about Nick's well-being. And that little clearing near the railroad he kept visiting during lunch? It was crazy, but Nick didn't seem to think anything of it. Frankly she was worried.

Gina couldn't see Nick well enough in the gloom to be sure, but she thought he rolled his eyes at her suggestion of ice cream.

"I don't think it's even open this late," he said. "Don't they close at nine?"

"They just switched to their summer hours so we have some time. Is that ok?"

Nick had finished his six-pack after he got home from work and then took a nap before he headed to the store to pick up his mom's prescription. So the buzz from earlier in the day was long gone. Getting another one started sounded good but wasn't absolutely necessary.

"Sure, let's go."

They walked slowly through Avon's deserted streets passing many homes where the blue glow of the living room television seemed to be the only light on in the house. Vehicle traffic on the streets was minimal. They were in no hurry. Anyone watching them would have seen two people who were obviously comfortable with each other, but even a casual observer would have guessed they were just friends and not a couple. There was no hand-holding or even incidental contact. Nick and Gina looked like two twenty-something buddies out for a stroll, and that's what they were.

There was no line at the Dairy Delite, but a few patrons were scattered among the wooden benches to the little building's rear enjoying cones, milkshakes and parfaits. One teenager was making quick work of a banana split, scooping spoonfuls of ice cream into his mouth so fast that Nick wondered briefly if he was trying to win a bet.

Nick ordered a chocolate cone and turned to ask Gina what she wanted.

"I'll get my own," she said.

"I'm already at the window. Another dollar and a half isn't going to break me, Gina. What do you want?"

"I'll get it."

For the second time in 20 minutes, Nick rolled his eyes at her. This time the lights were bright enough that she saw it clearly.

Gina got a cone too (vanilla) and joined Nick at a bench. Everyone else had gone home.

"What was that all about?" he asked as she sat down opposite him. "I can't buy you an ice cream cone?"

"This isn't a date, Nick. I can get my own. Do you buy Marty ice cream when you guys go out?"

"Me and Marty don't get ice cream when we go out," he said.

Now it was Gina's turn to roll her eyes.

"You know what I mean."

"Fine," he said. "Can we drop it?" Gina said nothing.

"When's the last time you were on a date anyway?" He smiled. Nick knew it had been months and was trying to lighten the mood.

"You really want to go there, Nick? I've been out more recently than you."

The truth was that neither Nick nor Gina had been on a real date for nearly a year, although Gina was right: She had dated more recently than Nick. On that occasion, about 11 months ago, she found out early in the evening that the guy (Art) had the worst breath she had ever encountered and his fingernails were long enough to warrant painting. She couldn't get away fast enough. When Nick inquired about the date on the phone the next day she simply said, "Don't ask."

Neither of them ever had anything approaching a steady boyfriend or girlfriend, even though Nick liked to point out that he and Aileen Nelson were exclusive for most of the third grade.

Casual friends of Gina's — she didn't have anything other than casual friends really, other than Nick — had suggested that spending so much time with Nick was giving off the wrong vibe. Other guys just assumed she and Nick were a couple because they spent so much time together. Gina replied by saying she didn't give a shit what anyone thought.

Nick chuckled as he worked on his cone. It was chilly and there was little need to worry about the ice cream melting, but he was kind of a neat freak in some ways and absolutely hated ice cream running across his knuckles.

He looked up after getting the ice cream safely back within the cone's borders where it belonged.

"So how have you been, you know, physically lately?" he asked.

Gina stopped mid-lick and looked over at him. She didn't have to ask what he meant.

"Come again?" She stared at him.

"You know what I mean."

"First you start in on me about dating and now you're going to ask about that."

"I'm just making conversation. Would you relax? I worry about you, that's all," he said. Nick resumed cleaning up his cone and immediately wished he could change the subject. Sometimes he just said stuff before he thought about it. He should have known better.

"I'm fine Nick. No need for you to worry. Seems to me you have your own issues, if you're looking for something to worry about."

About a week before, Nick and Gina had been having lunch at the Winky's restaurant in town when she had a seizure. Nick had seen them before, but that didn't make it any less scary. She didn't flop around on the floor, which was the image most people immediately associated with epilepsy. Her seizures were "petit mal" rather than "grand mal," and the result was that she would simply shut down for a couple of minutes. One second she was telling Nick about a new television show she had seen the night before and the next she was staring blankly straight ahead, all color gone from her face. After a few moments she began rocking slowly back and forth in the booth and mumbling quietly. Nick couldn't understand any of what she was saying.

Nick once had a conversation with Mrs. Marino about the seizures (and God help them both if Gina ever found out about that) and she told him that there was really nothing to be done if he was with Gina when it happened. The important thing was just to make sure she was stable so that she didn't hurt herself. The seizure would work itself out in a matter of a few minutes, she said.

"Ok, I can do that," he told her. "But can I ask you something?"

"Sure Nick."

"Why won't she talk about it? I mean, she doesn't even use the word seizure or epilepsy. And if I bring It up, she just about bites my head off," he said. Gina would only refer to her ailment as "my stomach thing" because at the onset of the seizures she would feel a fluttering in her gut. Nick knew this not from Gina herself but because her mom had filled him in.

"Sorry about that Nick," Mrs. Marino said. "She's always been that way about it since she was a little girl. She's embarrassed, I think, even though her dad and I have told her countless times that there's no reason to feel that way. It's not her fault that she has it. It breaks my heart."

Gina was on medication that, for the most part, kept the seizures under control. Nick had only been around her a handful of times when it happened over the years. It never got any less frightening, though.

A larger issue — and this was something Nick learned the hard way could absolutely, positively NOT be discussed — was Gina's driving. She was able to get a state-issued driver's license because of the meds, and there had never been any problems while she was behind the wheel, as far as Nick knew. It was obvious that Gina (maybe only subconsciously) and her parents tried to limit her driving time as much as possible. But still. Nick couldn't help but think that occasionally having seizures and occasionally driving a car were two things that were bound to overlap at some point. It was simple math. He thought to himself that it was a little like playing Russian roulette but instead of a lone bullet to worry about, this practice had the potential to hurt more people than just the shooter.

Maybe a lot more.

"OK, I'm sorry I brought it up," Nick said.

"No, I'm actually glad you did." She switched her cone from her left hand to her right and held her left out toward him. The cut he noticed back at the store was easily visible. It ran in almost a straight line from the middle of her palm to the space between her thumb and pointer finger. It was healing but was still red and puffy. "See this?"

"Did that happen while you were tackling that guy at the store?"

"No, Nick, it happened last week." She waited a beat, but he just looked at her.

"Friday night, when we were over at the Hillside. Any of this ringing a bell? Remember you hit that curb on the way home and flattened the tire?"

He did and he didn't. He remembered picking Gina up and driving to Conway, Avon's neighbor to the east. There was a bar in town called the Hillside Tavern that had buckets of Buds on the cheap Friday nights. He remembered getting there and he remembered that damn Chapin song playing on the jukebox at some point *"little boy blue and the man on the moon..."* but not much else. Of course he knew about the flat tire because it was in the trunk and the spare was on the car when he went out the next day. But how that all came to be he wasn't sure. And, to be honest, he didn't want to know. "So what's your point?" he asked. Nick was regretting bringing up her medical condition. He should have known it would give her the opening to steer the conversation around to his drinking. She had tried to bring it up a couple times lately, but he kept ducking.

"You say you're worried about me Nick, but I'm worried about you. And out of the two of us I think you've given me a lot more to worry about than the other way around. That thing with the nest? C'mon Nick. It's crazy."

"You don't know what it's like to have to work in that hellhole for eight hours, Gina. If I need a couple drinks to help me get through the day so what? No one is getting hurt."

A young couple was walking down the street a few feet away from the bench where Nick and Gina sat. The guy glanced in their direction. Nick realized the conversation was probably louder than he intended. He collected himself.

"You think I like working at that store with those idiot customers? I don't Nick. It's no fun but you don't see me out back by the Dumpsters chugging beers. That's not normal behavior."

"What are you saying, Gina? It seems like you want to say something so just go ahead and say it."

Gina looked up from her ice cream, but what he saw in her eyes wasn't anger or frustration. It was something a lot closer to pity, and that was much worse.

"You ready to go?" she asked.

"Yeah. I'll walk you home." He stood and glanced over at Gina, hoping for a little smile that would tell him everything was still ok. But she wasn't looking at him. Nick noticed a little stream of chocolate ice cream was running down his hand.

o o o

That last time anyone heard from Nevin Sampson was in April of 1975. He was a photojournalist working for UPI and had prodded and pushed his bosses until they finally relented and sent him to South Vietnam. It was as dangerous an assignment as there was anywhere on the planet at the time, but Nevin didn't care. He needed closure. He wanted to walk where Nate had walked and see what Nate had seen.

He was 31 years old in the fall of 1974 when he finally got to Southeast Asia, but he was 32 at the time of the Fall of Saigon six months later. His last letter to his family described the situation there as "extremely tense."

Thirty two. The same age that Nate was when he died in Da Nang 10 years earlier. Nick had mentioned to Gina once recently that he probably only had about seven years left to live because 32 seemed to be the magic number for the Sampson boys of Avon.

On December 12, 1974, the North Vietnamese Army launched a preliminary offensive to secure transportation routes along the Cambodian border and — maybe more importantly — to see how the United States would react. When the U.S. made it clear it would not come to South Vietnam's aid, the NVA moved ahead with its offensive.

The northern front of South Vietnam collapsed in early 1975, leading to a panicked exodus of American troops from the port of Da Nang back to Saigon. But UPI and other American news agencies retained journalists in the region even after the capture of the South Vietnamese capital city in late April.

Nevin's last letter, which his mom kept in a side table drawer close to the couch where she slept every night, said things were getting "dicey" but he sounded upbeat and implored his family not to worry.

"I'll be back home soon," he wrote. "Tell Nick I want to take another trip to Pocataw."

The letter arrived but Nevin never did. UPI eventually sent its condolences (and a bouquet of flowers) and said it lost touch with Nevin on April 15. None of its other reporters in the area ever saw him after that.

CHAPTER SEVEN

A few weeks after Nick and Gina shared cones at the Dairy Delite, Nick had a rare three-day break from work — Memorial Day weekend. The Saturday before the holiday was the traditional opening day for most of the businesses in Pocataw (although some had started opening their doors for the season on Mother's Day weekend in recent years) and Nick decided he would drive up for the day. There were a few shops that stayed open year-round but most catered strictly to the tourists that flocked to the little village from Memorial Day to Labor Day each year.

The town, whose name came from the body of water on which it sat, was so small it had no stop lights. Its main attraction (other than the lake) was a one-mile long, commercial stretch of road known to locals and visitors as "the strip." It featured gaming arcades, food stands and bars. Lots and lots of bars.

The Sampsons had spent a week in Pocataw each of the four summers that Nevin was in college. Ellen wanted all of them (other than Nate, who was in the service) to spend some time together before Nevin graduated and left home for good. He had made no secret of his desire to get away from Western Pennsylvania. Pocataw was relatively close to home, inexpensive and still gave the family some time at the beach, although a man-made lake in the northwest corner of the state was a long way from the Atlantic Ocean, both figuratively and geographically.

And while Nick still occasionally visited the town, (he had gone with Nevin once or twice too) the last of those whole-family trips took place in 1964. It was the year Nick turned 11.

Halfway through that week they got a knock on the cabin door and were stunned and elated to find Nate standing there wearing his military cammies and a huge smile. Ellen opened the door and shrieked when she saw her oldest son standing in the sun with his duffle bag over his shoulder. Her hands flew to her mouth as tears welled in her eyes. She was too stunned to move.

"Aren't you going to let me in?" Nate asked.

Hearing his voice unlocked her muscles, and Ellen flew down the steps and threw her arms around Nate. She

sobbed happy tears and squeezed him with all her
might. She didn't want to let go.

o o o

When Nick arrived early on that Saturday before
Memorial Day, the first stop he made was Jim's
Donuts. Jim's was probably the most well-known
establishment in town, and people drove in from
miles away to get the freshly-made donuts. The
shop seemed to pride itself on offering very few
varieties but making them exceptionally well.
Nick was partial to the crème-covered cake
donuts with rainbow-colored sprinkles on top. He
had heard rumors the "secret ingredient" that
separated Jim's crème from similar donuts made
by other establishments was marshmallow. He
grabbed two of them and a large, black coffee and
started walking to the state park that overlooked
the lake.

Pedestrian and vehicle traffic was still light at that
hour, but he knew by evening the town would be
packed. Nick passed at least four bars on the
short walk to the park. They were all closed. He
was planning to avoid them and hoped to be
headed back home before the village really got
jumping. He was far from believing he had any

sort of drinking problem (although Gina clearly wasn't as sure) but thought a sober Saturday couldn't hurt. It had been a while since he'd had one.

Instead, he thought Pocataw might be the right setting to do a little writing. He had no formal training and had never been paid a dime for anything he had written, but Nick privately thought he wasn't too bad at it. He had never shown any of the handful of short stories he'd written over the years to anyone and had no plans to do so anytime soon. Although he would never have admitted it — especially not to himself — he was hoping that rekindling his interest in writing would distract his mind from its growing obsession with alcohol. Part of him also wondered if maybe writing could someday be his ticket out of Kingston Bottling. But that was a goal for another day. For Saturday, he simply wanted to see if he could pick up the story he had started a few weeks before, and do it in a place that he always associated first and foremost with drinking.

He walked into the park and headed for a large pavilion that sat atop a little hill overlooking Lake

Pocataw. There were few boats out on the water yet, but — like the empty bars — he knew that would change as the day wore on. There were a dozen large picnic tables inside the little building. None were occupied. He sat down on one of the wooden benches that was badly in need of a fresh coat of paint and opened the manilla folder he had brought with him. Inside was a thin sheaf of yellow pages. At the top of the first one in the stack was a single word. "**Peter**," it read. And below that:

I have a friend named Peter. Peter lost his job about a year and a half ago. Lost probably isn't the right word, however, because Peter quit his job. It was no big deal. He didn't see eye to eye with management about something relatively trivial and so he left. It was a dead-end job anyway so, again, it was no big deal. The problem is that now it has been a year and a half and Peter doesn't have another job yet. Peter hasn't looked for another job yet. He just sits home all day in the house where he grew up and waits. His mother still lives there, so she waits too. She is patient with him and doesn't hassle Peter about finding a job.

What I find myself wondering is what, exactly, he is waiting for. On a weekly basis he waits for the weekend. On the weekends, he drinks. A lot. On the larger scale, however, I'm not sure what he is waiting for. A sign from God perhaps. Or maybe he's waiting for the courage to kill himself.

Nick read through what he had written and thought about what should come next. He already knew what the last line of this little story would be, but he had to figure out how to get there. *Do real writers struggle with this stuff?*, he wondered. Probably not. He looked out over the water and waited for the words to come. After a couple of minutes, they did.

As I said, Peter is a friend. A very close friend. So what am I to do? Talk to him about it?

I've tried. Peter is a very private person and seems to be very much offended by my attempts to help. I've talked to his mom about him as well. She doesn't know what to do either. She knows something has to be done, but not specifically what.

Nick stopped and looked over the newest paragraph. He didn't love it. The right feeling was there, but the wording was clunky. He put the pen down and took a big gulp of his coffee. He had eaten one of the donuts on the walk to the park and debated eating the other. He decided to save it for later.

He looked out toward the strip and noticed a girl walking his way. She was wearing a bright yellow sundress and a wide-brimmed hat of the exact same color. He guessed she was walking over for a better look at the lake. The park had the best views in town

He looked down at his story and debated which direction to take Peter's story next. Things were not going to end well for Peter. Of that much, he was sure. He picked up the pen and started to write when he noticed the girl in the yellow dress had not veered around the pavilion and moved on toward the lake as he expected. She was approaching him.

He stopped writing, looked up and smiled. Up close, he could see that she was a little older than he originally thought. Maybe 21 or 22. And she was gorgeous. Nick watched as she approached his table.

"Hi there," she said. "Sorry to bother you. I can see you're busy."

Nick looked briefly back down at his story and closed the folder. "No problem. I'm stuck anyway. You come to check out the lake? It's beautiful out there today."

"Actually no, although you're right. It's spectacular today. But my car has a flat." She pointed toward the park's little parking lot over her shoulder. He noticed her nails were bright red. "Any chance you could help?"

Nick looked down at the folder again and then back up at the stranger (wondering briefly if she had drunkenly hit a curb to flatten her tire too). The whole thing seemed dreamlike. Girls that looked like her did not talk to Nick Sampson, even if it was just to ask for a favor. He must have hesitated a second too long because she started to backtrack.

"Look, never mind. I shouldn't have bothered you. I'm sorry. I just have no idea about cars. Have a good one." She turned to walk away when Nick snapped out of his daze.

"No, wait," he said and stood up. He noticed she was almost as tall as he was. "Sorry. Sure, I can help. It's no problem." He stuck out his hand. "I'm Nick." "Michelle," she said.

She smiled.

o o o

About 30 minutes later, Nick had the spare tire in place and was pretty sure it wouldn't fall off. His new friend Michelle had professed to knowing little about autos, and the same was certainly true of Nick. But he kept his mouth shut on the topic and thought he did a passable job with the tire. He stowed the flat and the jack in the trunk and walked around to the front of the car where Michelle was standing.

"You're all set," he said. "But I wouldn't go flying around on that spare." She flashed that smile again and Nick's mind went blank.

"No worries. I live just up the road. Thanks again Nick."

In all the years Nick had been going to Pocataw, he didn't think he had ever run into one of the locals unless they were working in one of the bars or restaurants. Her comment caught him off guard. He had just assumed she was a tourist.

"Oh, well that's good," he said. He didn't know what to do so he just stuck out his hand.

"Well, see ya."

She reciprocated and then climbed behind the wheel. Nick watched her the whole way in.

After she pulled out, Nick headed back toward the pavilion and his short story. He noticed a softball game had broken out on the overgrown baseball field that sat on the far side of the park. It looked like it might be a family affair because the teams were comprised of young children, older adults and everything in between. As he walked, he watched a left-handed batter rip a pitch over the right fielder's head. The kid tore around the bases while a girl who might have been his older sister chased the ball.

Nick sat back down and opened the folder containing his story again. He read the last line several times and tried to figure out where to take Peter from there. Eventually, he began to write.

I am not a psychologist. I do, however, have some theories about what is ailing Peter. His upbringing undoubtedly has a lot to do with it. His parents did the best they knew how, but in Peter's case it just wasn't good enough. He was allowed to float through school with no plans for the future. Granted, many kids that age are unsure of what they want out of life. But his parents never even approached the subject with him. They never asked him if he planned to go to college. They never asked him if he planned to get a job. They just left him alone in their own loving way, and Peter drifted into oblivion.

At one point he got up and walked out of the pavilion to get a closer look at the lake.

The breeze off the water carried a faint fishy smell that he would always associate with Pocataw. The sun felt good on his face. He was hoping for some inspiration but couldn't find it.

Eventually he walked back and wrote a little more, then finished the last of the (cold) coffee. He looked at his watch and was shocked to see how much of the day had already drained away. Part of it was spent changing Michelle's tire, but he had lost most of the early afternoon trying to find the right words for the story. It was maddening.

He was getting hungry, and although he briefly considered just eating the second donut he'd bought that morning, he decided to walk over to Ed's for a slice of pizza.

With folder in hand, Nick left the park and strolled down the strip. He noticed how much more crowded it was than when he entered the park that morning. And the numbers would only grow as the day wore on.

He didn't know anyone in town, so he at first paid no attention when he heard someone calling his name. *Must be another Nick,* he thought. But there was something familiar about the voice. He walked on and again heard someone calling. "Hey Nick, over here!" He looked out toward the street and saw Michelle. She was parked at the curb and leaning across the front seat of her car to yell out the rolled-down, passenger-side window.

He walked over and put his hands on the window frame.

"Don't tell me. The tire fell off?"

Michelle actually laughed out loud. She had a cute laugh. "Not yet," she said. "Where are you headed? You need a lift?"

"No just going down to Ed's." He pointed and then realized how dumb he probably looked. As if she didn't know where Ed's was.

He starred at her, and she seemed to be debating what she was going to say next. He pushed off the car, gave a little wave and was about to move on when she stopped him again.

"I was thinking about getting a drink," she said. "You game?"

A flurry of images rolled through Nick's head like reels in a slot machine. When they stopped, he could see Gina sitting across from him at the Dairy Delite a few weeks earlier.

"I'm fine Nick. No need for you to worry," she had said. *"Seems to me you have your own issues, if you're looking for something to worry about."*

He wanted to tell Michelle no. He wanted to say he was getting the pizza, heading to his car and driving home to Avon.

He even opened his mouth. But nothing came out.

"Nick?"

He blinked and Gina was gone.

Michelle was still there.

"Sure," he said. "That sounds great."

Part Two

The Body

CHAPTER EIGHT

"I need to use the bathroom. And I'll get the next round while I'm back there." Nick stood and started walking between the closely-placed tables across the Hillside Tavern's long, rectangular barroom. Gina watched him closely. Only about half of the tables had customers. *Pretty thin for a Friday night*, she thought. Nick worked his way toward the back of the smoky room where the bar itself sat. To the right of that, a short hallway led to the public bathrooms.

Gina thought there was a little bit of a weave working its way into Nick's stride. It wasn't obvious, but it was there if you looked closely. They had arrived at the bar about two hours earlier and had gone through two buckets of Buds. Each bucket contained six, 12-ounce beers, but she knew that he had been outpacing her about two to one. She guessed he'd had 8 beers so far. It was only 11 o'clock, but Gina thought she'd need to get him out of there soon.

Their conversation at the Dairy Delite was still a week away, and Gina was thinking of how best to address his drinking. It would take a delicate touch, and that was certainly not her usual style. Still, something had to be said.

The problem was that such a conversation couldn't take place while he was drinking (duh) or even on a day after, when he was feeling like crap. Nick was typically pretty irritable with even a mild hangover, and she avoided him on those days if she could. But eliminating the days when he was either drinking or had the night before didn't leave many opportunities to talk. *Fewer and fewer all the time*, she thought.

Nick walked up to the bar and motioned to Tony, the bartender. Tony was chatting with two girls who looked like they wouldn't see their 21st birthdays for another year or two. IDs were rarely checked at the Hillside. He clearly wasn't busy.

"Another bucket?" he said as Nick approached.

"No, gimme three singles. Hold two here. I'll be back in a sec."

Tony reached under the bar and pulled three Buds out of a large cooler. He placed them on the scarred bar top and popped off the bottle caps. Nick dropped a 5-dollar bill next to them and grabbed one of the beers. As casually as he could, he turned his head to make sure Gina wasn't watching. All clear. He took the bottle and quickly walked back to the men's room. Surprisingly, he didn't need to pee. He walked into the nearest stall and closed the door behind him. Nick chugged the beer in one long pull. He set the empty on top of the toilet tank, let out a huge belch and walked out into the bathroom.

Nick declined Tony's offer for another bucket not for economic reasons or because he thought his drinking session was coming to an end soon. It wasn't. Instead, he wanted to get home and drink the way he wanted to. Out in public — and especially around Gina — he felt the need to pace himself in a way that he didn't when he was home alone in his room. Gina would have laughed (uneasily) at the notion that drinking eight beers in two hours was a slow pace. But for Nick it was.

He walked back over to the bar and grabbed the two remaining Buds. He noticed Tony was already back between the two coeds at the other end of the bar. He chuckled. Nick was working his way back to Gina, trying to do a passable job of appearing relatively sober as he weaved through the patrons, when his right foot came down on the toes of a guy sitting at one of the tables.

"Hey! Fuck! Watch where you're going!" the guy yelled.

Nick turned back, a beer in each hand. "Oh sorry, man. It was an accident." He again started toward Gina, halfway back in the room, when he heard the guy say "fucking drunk."

Nick stopped again. He turned. "What'd you say?"

"I said you're fucking drunk," the guy repeated, even louder. He started getting out of his seat. "Did you hear me that time?"

From her vantage point, Gina couldn't see exactly what was happening but there was obviously a problem. She was out of her seat in a flash and positioned herself between Nick and the (burly) stranger. She looked the guy in the eyes and asked what happened.

"Your drunk boyfriend here stepped on my fucking foot. Might have broke my toes," the guy said.

"I said I was sorry, and you better stop calling me drunk," Nick said. He was pushing up against Gina but was in no real hurry to get at the guy. But there was no way he was going to back down. Gina quickly looked for a way to de-escalate the situation and found inspiration in Nick's hands. She grabbed both beers from him and put them on the table.

"A peace offering," she said, and started pulling Nick back to their table.

She sat down but noticed that Nick kept moving toward the front door. She called, but he kept walking.

Gina ran and caught up with him in the parking lot. She put a hand on his arm to stop him. "What are you doing, Nick? We're leaving?"

"Well you gave away my beer and I'm not buying any more. I'm going home, but feel free to stay." He used his key to open the car door and started to climb in.

"First of all, you're my ride. And second of all, you're in no condition to drive, Nick. Stop acting like an asshole. Move." Gina started trying to slide past him into the driver's seat, but Nick wouldn't budge.

"Uh, no. It's my car and I'm driving. It's only 10 minutes. I could do that in my sleep."

He climbed in but didn't start the car. He sat there with the door open. "Coming?" "You can be such a dick, Nick," she said.

"Hey, that rhymes," he said.

Gina walked around the back of Nick's car — an 8-year-old Chevy Chevelle — and climbed into the passenger seat. He was ready to put the car in reverse when Gina put her hand on his arm. "Wait, Nick. Can we talk for a minute?" He just sat there starring out the windshield. She wasn't sure he heard her.

"Nick..."

"Did I ever tell you about the time my dad almost punched me?"

She was caught off guard by the direction the conversation had taken and sat there dumbstruck for a minute. Nick almost never talked about his father.

"Uh, I don't think so," she said. "When was this?"

"I must have been 10. It was just a couple of years before he...you know." Gina waited, unsure what to say.

The Hillside had two speakers mounted on telephone poles in the parking lot so that when house bands were playing inside, the music could still be enjoyed by those coming and going. When there was no band, the system was hooked up to the old jukebox that sat in the corner. Bob Seger had just finished singing "Still the Same" when Harry Chapin began crooning about his son who was born just the other day.

"Oh Jesus you have to be kidding me. Not now," Nick said.

"What?"

"This song. I can't get away from it."

Gina had to strain to hear it. Eventually she realized it was "Cat's in the Cradle," but she wasn't sure what significance it had to Nick. She ran the lyrics through her head and then it hit her. Oh boy.

Another car pulled into the lot, and a young couple headed into the bar. The girl playfully jumped on the guy's back for a brief piggyback ride then dismounted before they walked in.

Gina was afraid the moment was passing. She wanted to hear the story about Nick and his dad.

"You were saying?" Nick took a deep breath. "My dad was playing on the mill's softball team that summer. He was actually pretty good, although he couldn't run. He'd crush the ball and then lumber around the bases. It was pretty funny but pretty cool too. Just to see that side of him. It was easy to imagine what he must have been like as a kid."

"Anyway, he slid into third base one night and broke his foot. They wanted to take him to the hospital, but he refused. He hobbled around on it for a couple days until he had no choice but to get it taken care of. He couldn't work."

Nick paused. He was staring straight ahead through the dirty windshield at a scene that took place 15 years before. Gina lightly put her left hand on his leg. There was no one else around.

She was about to prompt him again when he picked up the story.

"So he was sitting on the glider on our back porch one day right before he got the cast on. You remember that old green one?" She nodded, but he didn't see it. "He had the bad foot out in front of him a little. I ran out the back door — I don't even remember why I was running — and I stepped on his foot."

Gina understood. The incident with the guy in the bar had brought the memory back up.

"It was a total accident. Just one of those stupid things." Nick shook his head and looked over at her. "He screamed and cocked his fist back. Like he was going to hit me. I think it was just instinctive, but I'll never forget the look he gave me. Never." "Oh Nick, I'm sorry. I didn't know." She patted his leg.

"He seemed to realize what was happening and put his fist down. I think he felt bad, but he never said anything about it. We never talked about it."

"Like you said, Nick, he reacted to the pain without thinking. He would have reacted the same way to anyone who hurt him like that. I'm sure he felt terrible about it."

Nick shifted in his seat, closed the door and started to roll down the driver's side window. "But that look on his face," he said. "It was pure hatred."

He put the key in and turned over the ignition. The sound of the engine coming to life snapped Gina out of the past and into the problem she had in the present.

"You can't drive, Nick. You had at least eight beers. And those are just the ones that I know of." He blushed.

"C'mon Nick, switch with me. Let me drive."

"You can stay in or you can get out, but I'm driving. I put the window down so I'll get some air." He looked at her for a couple of seconds. Gina sighed and shook her head. It was a short drive, and God knew he had done it before.

"Fine," she said.

Nick put the car in reverse and pulled out of the parking spot. Gina noticed that he never looked back.

Pocataw had no shortage of bars, and Nick and Michelle decided on Ye Olde Pub. It sat on the eastern end of the strip. Few of the other popular tourist spots were that far out from the center of town, so the place mainly catered to locals.

Nick grabbed two beers and joined her at a table in the farthest corner from the door.

The place wasn't quite packed, but it was busier than it normally would be on a late Saturday afternoon. As he walked toward Michelle, Nick thought that in a couple of hours it would be standing room only.

He set a beer in front of Michelle and took his seat on the opposite side of the table. Nick was prepared for the usual "getting-to-know-you" questions and answers and was taken completely off guard when the first thing she said was "tell me a joke."

"Come again?"

"You heard me. Tell me a joke."

"The only two things you know about me are my first name and that I'm a shitty tirechanger and this is what you start with? I guess I'm not dating enough these days. Is this the new standard opening line?"

She just smiled. "I'm waiting."

Nick was not much of a jokester, and his mind reeled as he tried to come up with something. After a few seconds, he remembered a letter he had read in a magazine a few weeks before. It was supposedly sent to a middle school principal's office after the school had sponsored a luncheon for the elderly. An old lady won a new radio at the lunch as a door prize and was writing to say thank you.

Nick tried to remember the exact wording, which was critical for the joke to come off right. He gave Michelle the background information about the "alleged" correspondence and began. "The letter said..."

God bless you for the beautiful radio I won at your recent senior citizens' luncheon. I am 84 years old and live at the Safety Harbor Assisted Home for the Aged. All of my family has passed away. I am all alone now and it's nice to know that someone is thinking of me. God bless you for your kindness to an old forgotten lady. My roommate is 95 and always had her own radio, but before I received one, she would never let me listen to hers, even when she was napping. The other day her radio fell off the nightstand and broke into a lot of pieces. It was awful and she was in tears. She asked me if she could listen to mine, and I said fuck you.

Nick thought the joke was pretty funny (which was probably why he remembered it so well), but he was still surprised by Michelle's reaction. As soon as the words "fuck you" were out of Nick's mouth, she spat a mouthful of beer all over him and laughed so loud that people across the bar took notice. The fact that beer was dripping off of Nick's nose only made her laugh harder.

Nick chuckled to himself and thought maybe she was onto something with the idea of using a joke as a conversation ice-breaker.

After a couple of minutes, Michelle began to regain control of herself.

"No good huh?" Nick deadpanned. "Let me think of a different one."

CHAPTER NINE

Gina buckled her seatbelt and said a silent prayer as Nick began driving home from the Hillside. She knew it was stupid to get in the car with him, but there were few options, and they all seemed just as bad. She didn't want to call her parents for a ride because of the conversation that would surely ensue. They had no idea about Nick's drinking, and she wanted to keep it that way. There was really no one else to call. Walking was out of the question. Should she call a cab? That was probably the best solution, but she quickly dismissed it because she had no experience dealing with taxis and didn't want to learn on the fly (*did they even operate that late at night?*). Plus, she had no idea what it would cost.

She looked over at Nick and was stunned to see a 16-ounce beer in his hand. *What the hell?* He must have grabbed it from underneath his seat while she wasn't looking. But how did he do it so quickly? She immediately pictured a gunslinger in some old Western movie reaching into his holster and his hand emerging a split second later holding a gun. But maybe this time the barrel was pointed toward her.

"Nick, what are you doing? Where did you get that?" He took a pull of the beer and ignored her.

At least he's watching the road, she thought.

The trip was relatively short, and the roads were mostly deserted. Gina was starting to believe Nick would be able to navigate his way home when the car suddenly drifted to the left, crossed the center line and struck the curb on the far side. The contact jolted Nick awake, and he quickly corrected and pulled the car back into the right lane.

Gina shrieked then scolded herself for not watching him more closely. One second he was awake and the next he was not.

"God damn it Nick you fell asleep! You could have killed us!"

He had dropped the can on the floor near his feet, and beer was puddling on the carpet.

"I'm fine," he said.

But the car was not. Both Nick and Gina could tell immediately that something was wrong. There was no traffic on the road, and Nick started looking for somewhere to pull off. About a quarter of a mile down the road, Gina spotted a lighted parking lot on the right.

"There Nick," she pointed. "Pull in."

He steered the car into the lot and killed the engine.

"Nice work," she said. Gina was still shaken from the incident but didn't want Nick to see it. She wanted him to know she was more pissed off than anything else. "You flattened the tire. Can you change it?"

Nick gingerly climbed out of the car and walked around to the trunk. He put the key in and opened it. Then he just stood there, rocking on his feet.

Gina turned and looked over the headrest and out the rear window, but the trunk lid was blocking her view. She couldn't see what Nick was doing. She expected to hear the sounds of him digging out the spare tire and jack, but there was silence coming from the rear of the car.

A minute passed and she got out to see what he was doing. She found him standing there, just starring into the trunk.

"Nick?"

"Huh?"

"Are you gonna change the tire?" She looked at him more closely. His eyes were half shut. "Are you ok?" It was a rhetorical question. Clearly, he was not.

A line from those old black-and-white, Laurel and Hardy movies sprung into Gina's mind. *This is another fine mess you've gotten us into.*

Fuming, Gina brushed past Nick and began digging the spare tire and bumper jack out of the trunk. They were buried under a lot of debris — grey, oil-stained overalls that had the Kingston logo on the breast pocket, some fast-food wrappers and the remnants of what might have once been a sleeping bag among it — so it took her a few seconds. She set the (bald) tire and the lug wrench on the ground and grabbed the base of the jack stand. As she pulled, it caught on something, and her hand scraped across one of the sharp edges.

"Fuck!"

She pulled back and looked at her hand. It was hard to see in the dim light, but it was obvious there was a thin line across her palm that had not been there before. The blood looked black in the darkness.

"This is great." She looked at Nick. He just stood there, rocking back and forth from his heels to his toes. Gina didn't know it, but he looked much like she did on the day he spotted her having a seizure when they were kids. "I'm bleeding Nick." With that, he seemed to come back to himself, at least a little.

"Hang on," he said, and walked around to the driver's side. While she waited, Gina took her first good look at their surroundings since Nick had limped the car into the lot.

"Oh for the love of God," she said.

The car was sitting in the outer reaches of the parking area of another bar. She had missed the sign (The Oyster Bar) when they pulled in. It was unlit, as if most of the tavern's customers didn't need to be reminded that it was there. She wondered briefly if the place was even open.

There was a neon beer sign in the window, but she couldn't see any other vehicles in the lot.

Nick returned and handed her a handkerchief that he must have found inside the car. It wasn't exactly clean, but she thought it would do the trick and wrapped it tightly around her hand. He was also holding another beer. Gina wondered how many more he had inside the car.

Gina had never changed a flat but assumed it would be fairly easy to figure out. But now her hand was bleeding, and more than anything she wanted to get the two of them home as quickly as possible

"I'm gonna walk over there and see if someone can help," she told him. "You stay here." The last thing she wanted was for Nick to get inside another bar.

"Why, I can change it," he said. His words were running together.

"Why don't you go back in the car and relax, Nick. I'll be right back." She didn't wait for a response and headed toward the little cinder-block building. As she got closer, Gina understood why she hadn't seen any other cars.

Nick had actually entered the establishment's rear lot. The main entrance was on the other side of the building, and there was a smattering of cars and pickup trucks haphazardly parked near the door on that side.

Having no idea what she was going to say when she got in there, Gina opened the door and walked into a small entryway that led to a long, narrow room. There were two pool tables along the left side and a long bar down the right. There were probably 20 people in the place including a handful of middle-aged men standing around the pool tables holding long, wooden cues. It was probably just her imagination, but conversations seemed to dry up as soon as she entered. She could hear the clink of pool balls on one of the tables. Many of the bar's patrons seemed to be looking right at her. *Here we go,* she thought.

"Hey, hi. Uh, excuse me. I was wondering if I could get some help. I have a flat tire and I hurt my hand." She held it up in case they didn't believe her. "I know it's a lot to ask, but could someone change it for me? I'd really appreciate it." She immediately regretted the last line, thinking it may have suggested something she certainly didn't mean to imply.

She knew she wasn't imagining the silence in the place at that point. All eyes were on her. No one responded. Ten seconds went by that felt like an hour. No one moved. Gina was getting creeped out and started thinking the flat tire and Nick's condition might be the least of her worries.

Just as she was turning to go (telling herself not to run), a guy of about 30 stepped away from the nearest of the pool tables. He had a Steelers baseball cap on his head and wore a black T-shirt that said "The Real Thing" in red block letters. Without a word, he walked past her and headed out to the parking lot. Gina stood there for another second and then followed him out.

o   o   o

The next morning, Nick remembered little beyond stepping on the stranger's foot inside the Hillside. He had (again) drank himself into a blackout, so his memories of everything that followed that heated exchange were a blur. He was coming to understand that those blank spots were one of the fun side effects of drinking yourself into oblivion. You were dependent on those who had been with you to fill you in on what had happened.

Or what you had done.

Gina never told Nick what happened at the Oyster Bar, other than the brief recap she gave him during their conversation at the Dairy Delite. And no one was in the

McDonalds parking lot where Nick's night ultimately came to an end. Well, no one other than the homeless guy who was passing through.

At least until the police showed up.

Gina thanked the stranger for changing the tire and poured Nick into the passenger seat. By then, he was well beyond arguing that he was ok to drive. He made a couple of attempts to pull the keys out of the front pocket of his jeans, but Gina eventually dug them out herself.

She drove the rest of the way to Nick's house and parked his car on the street. Gina walked around, opened Nick's door and helped him out. He was unsteady on his feet. She eventually got him onto the front porch and considered ringing the bell.

By that point, he seemed to be coming around (maybe the brief nap had rejuvenated him) and she saw no point in waking Mrs. Sampson if she didn't have to.

Gina watched as he opened the door and went inside. She stood on the sidewalk for a minute and wondered how Nick's drinking had escalated so quickly. He had always liked beer, but in the past few months things had spiraled out of control. He was no longer drinking to have a good time.

Often now, he seemed to be drinking because he had no choice.

She started walking home.

Two minutes later, Nick emerged from the front door and headed in the opposite direction. He had watched and waited until Gina walked away. He was hungry and needed a beer. Nick had lost track of how many beers remained in the six-pack he had stashed under the car seat earlier in the day but thought there was a chance there might be one left. He got down on his knees and rummaged around until he struck gold.

One soldier still standing.

He smiled.

Nick walked, beer in hand, toward Avon's commercial district. It wasn't a long walk. The streets were empty. He turned a corner and saw the bright gold "M" of the McDonalds sign and immediately grew hopeful that the restaurant was still open, despite the late (or early) hour. As he got closer, though, he could see that the interior lights were mostly out. The place was closed.

But Nick was undeterred. He walked over to the nearest entrance and yanked on the big silver handle. It didn't budge. He yanked again. And again. All he wanted was a crumby cheeseburger or two. Was that too much to ask? He left the door and walked over to the large window that looked into the dining room. He cupped his hands against the glass to cut the glare from the parking lot lights. There was no one inside.

He stepped back and took a gulp from the beer. He was trying to solve the problem of how to get food from the locked restaurant, but his thinking was muddled. There had to be a way. The food was in there. Why couldn't he have it?

As he stood there, a guy approached from the drive-thru lane and moved toward Nick. The guy's clothes were frayed in many places and outright ripped in others, and his long, straggly locks had not encountered shampoo (or a comb) in a coon's age. Nick immediately thought *Brownie*, but it wasn't. Even in his current condition, Nick could see the guy was wearing a tattered trench coat rather than Brownie's Marine uniform. As Nick watched, the hobo stopped and pulled a huge wad of napkins out of his coat pocket. He separated one of them from the pile and violently blew his nose. The bum absently dropped the used napkin on the ground and peeled off another. He wadded that one up and shoved it first up one nostril and then the other. Then that napkin joined the first at his feet. He repeated the process over and over — one napkin for a blow job, another shoved almost up into his brain cavity — for what seemed like 15 minutes. When he was finally done, the guy put the remaining unused napkins back into his pocket and walked on toward the street, kicking a few of the dropped napkins as he went.

What the fuck was that? Nick thought. *This town really is going to hell.* The brief diversion was over, but Nick's problem remained: He needed food. He returned to the window and again cupped his hands around his face. This time he could see a man inside pushing a yellow mop bucket on wheels. Nick immediately knocked on the window with the almost-empty beer can. The guy looked up.

"Hey can you open the door?" Nick yelled.

The guy ignored him and kept moving toward the back of the restaurant.

"Hey!" Nick screamed and again pounded on the window with the can. The glass shook in its frame and the can folded in the middle.

"We're closed!" the guy yelled. "Come back tomorrow!"

Nick couldn't make out what the janitor was saying and didn't care. He just wanted inside, and the guy was making no movement toward the door. After Nick's next assault on the glass, the guy had seen enough. He dialed 911.

o o o

The responding officer found Nick lying flat on his back below the drive-thru window. Both arms were outstretched above his head, and an empty beer can lay on its side just beyond his right hand.

The cop, Officer Murdoch, shook Nick for nearly a minute before he started to come around. He looked dazed and his eyes were as red as the cardboard case the empty Stroh's can had undoubtedly come from. He helped Nick into the back of the car and asked him where he lived. It took Nick a minute, but he eventually remembered his address. The cop was happy the house was only a few blocks away. He didn't want the guy in his patrol car any longer than he had to be. He suspected his passenger had puking in his future.

The officer pulled to the curb in front of the Sampson house and turned back to Nick.

"This is your stop, pal."

Nick got out and shut the door. He walked up the front steps and into the house.

He never looked up, so he didn't see his mom in the upstairs window.

CHAPTER TEN

After his third beer with the lovely Michelle, Nick knew he had a problem.

Well, he had several problems — if he was being honest — but one was more pressing at that moment than the others: He was soon approaching the point where driving home (safely) was out of the question, and he had nowhere to stay in Pocataw. He had not planned on staying overnight. He had not planned on drinking. He had not planned on meeting the beautiful yet unattached (and seemingly at least somewhat interested in Nick Sampson) Michelle Funaro.

He told her he had to go to the bathroom but instead ducked out the rear door of the pub and ran next door. If bars were the number one industry in Pocataw (they were) then cheap motels were number two. Most of those in town had been built a decade or two earlier and followed one of two popular designs. There were the almost-always twostory "L"-shaped establishments and the usually three-story "U"-

shaped motels. The latter models often featured a swimming pool right in the middle of the U.

One of the outliers was the Poolside Motel, which sat next to Ye Olde Pub. It was a long, box-like structure and, at four stories, was the tallest building in town. Nick would have preferred to stay on the western end of the strip where the places were typically cheaper, but he didn't want to be away from Michelle any longer than necessary, and he didn't want her to know he was just then booking a room.

It might give her the wrong idea. Or the right idea, depending on how the rest of the night went.

He paid for the room, grabbed the key and hustled back to the bar. When he walked in, he noticed that the table he and Michelle had been sharing was empty. Her purse had been hanging on the back of her chair, and it was gone too. *Way to go Nick*, he thought. *She was just waiting for an opening to high-tail it out of here and you handed it to her on a silver platter. She's gone, and she ain't coming back.*

Nick resumed his seat at the table and took a drink of his beer. Part of him was sort of relieved that she had left. There would be no awkward parting now (either tonight or in the morning), and if he got some coffee into his system, he might be able to cancel his room, get his money back and hit the road after all. For some reason, an image of Gina's face popped into his head along with that last thought.

"Oh, there you are. I had to use the restroom too, but I didn't see you back there. I thought maybe you ran out on me," Michelle said with a smile as she sat down at the table. The look on her face told Nick that she didn't really believe he had left for good. *The next man who walks out in the middle of a date with me will be the first,* that look said.

"Haha no, there was a line in the men's room. Sorry it took me so long." He took another swig. "So where were we? I forget what we were talking about."

She took a drink and set the bottle back down but in a slightly different spot. There was a ring of water on the table where the bottle had been sitting. Michelle began running her pointer finger through it. She didn't look up.

"I started thinking maybe your conscience got the best of you and you had to get back to your girlfriend." With that, she did look at him. "Before this goes any further, I really need to ask you about that. Is there a girlfriend to get back to, Nick?"

Say no, Nick, the voice inside his head demanded. *Put her mind at ease, and do it quick.*

Because it was the truth. He had no girlfriend. He *never* had a girlfriend.

And yet, he noticed that his mouth was not relaying that message to Michelle.

"Nick?"

"Uh no, not really," he finally said. "I don't."

She started running her finger through the water ring again.

"That's a strange way to answer, Nick. It seems to me that's a pretty black and white issue." She let out a sigh. "Anything other than a straight 'no' sounds a lot like 'yes' to me."

She stood up and grabbed her purse off the chair back. "Thanks for the beer, Nick. And for the help with the car earlier. Be careful driving home."

Say something! that interior voice screamed at him. *Don't let her get away!*

But he just sat there as she walked toward the exit.

He couldn't take his eyes off her

He wasn't the only one.

o o o

A few minutes later, Nick followed her out. He was not surprised to see that the crowd on the strip had grown considerably since he'd gone inside. The town was jumping. Cars sat bumper to bumper in both directions, but no one cared. The idea was to be seen. Music blared from many of the open windows. From a Malibu idling in front of him, Nick heard Lindsey Buckingham singing about lonely days and going your own way.

Loving you isn't the right thing to

do How can I ever change things

that I feel?

Nick walked down the strip.

He had a beer in each hand. One was his and the other was Michelle's. *Waste not want not,* he thought, and chuckled to himself.

He briefly considered that half-formed plan from a few minutes earlier of grabbing a coffee and hitting the road. But who was he kidding? He wasn't going anywhere.

After a couple more hours walking up and down the strip, stopping in bars now and then for a beer (and to use the bathroom), Nick ended up on a bench in front of Ed's with a burger in his hands. He was exhausted. The crowd was finally thinning, and another Saturday night on the strip was winding down.

Nick took the burger and a beer and walked back to the Poolside. He found his room on the fourth floor overlooking the pool. Nick opened the sliding glass door and walked out onto the little balcony. He'd never stayed at the Poolside, and the view from up there was actually kind of cool. Almost worth the price of the room.

He went back inside and closed the slider. He propped himself on the bed and was asleep almost immediately.

He dreamed.

And he was back at the (bottomless) pond that sat on the other side of the (ancient) forest from the old hotel. The night was black as pitch. Everything was the same as the previous time he'd been there. Except for one: This time, Nick was aware that he was dreaming.

I never have recurring dreams, he thought as he stood there at the water's edge. What's happening?

In room 404 of the Poolside Motel in the vacation town of Pocataw, Nick Sampson lay perfectly still on the old mattress. He did not move a muscle, but a single bead of sweat ran down his forehead.

I need to wake up, he thought. I need to get out of here. *He would not look across the pond.*

Nothing moved. The night was utterly without sound. Until it wasn't.

"Come," the creature on the far side of the water again whispered.

Nick shook his head, but paralyzing fear prevented him from giving voice to the negative response that remained stuck in his throat. He knew he had to wake up, but in the meantime he had to get away from the pond. The idea of heading back to that (haunted, it's haunted) hotel was dreadful, but anything was better than standing in the presence of the thing in the distance.

He turned to run but found his feet were as locked up as his voice. He couldn't move.

In room 404, Nick thrashed and kicked. He rolled over and fell to the floor but did not wake up.

"Nick....come..."

Against his will, he again looked over at the source of that (dead, it's dead) voice. A bony finger was beckoning him from across the water.

Nick looked down and was shocked to see that his feet were moving but not toward the hotel as he intended. He was headed into the pond. He fought against the movement but was unable to stop his legs. One halting step after another, and Nick's bare toes soon touched the water. It was as cold as the infinity of space.

With all his might, Nick tried to stop his advance. His left foot moved out over the water. It landed on the surface but did not penetrate. The right foot followed, and Nick was standing on the water's surface.

And still that (dead) finger beckoned him forward.

A dozen more steps and Nick was standing in the middle of the pond. He thought that if he couldn't stop himself from crossing the rest of the water and had to face that figure, he would surely go mad.

He took another grudging step forward. Two.

And then he fell through the surface.

His breath caught in his chest and he tried desperately to stop his descent. The water chilled him to the bone. He tried to kick toward the surface, but his legs felt as if cinder blocks were attached to them.

He continued to sink.

He looked down and saw the bottom was quickly approaching. His mind whirled. He decided he would push off the lakebed and try to reach the surface before his burning lungs ran out of air. A moment later, his feet landed on the sandy bottom. Nick bent his legs and thrust upward with all his might.

Two unseen hands clamped onto his ankles like vices. He flailed in the murky depths and expelled the last of his air. His eyes bulged. He screamed...

People sleeping in the units on both sides of room 404 snapped awake at the sound of his shouts.

Still on the floor, Nick awoke to a vison he would remember for the rest of his life.

o o o

When he was 10, Nick's best friend Jack once told him that if you died in a dream you would also die in real life. Jack said that any time you were about to dream-die, your brain would automatically kick into self-preservation mode and wake you up. Because if it didn't...

Where he had gained that knowledge was murky, but Jack backed it up by telling Nick that he, Jack, had once dreamt he was falling from the sky. But just before his body slammed into the earth, he snapped awake.

"One second later and I'd be dead," Jack said. "Ask anyone. It's true."

"You're full of it, Jack. Who told you that?"

"Think about it, Nicky. Have you ever died in a dream?"

Nick had to admit that he couldn't think of a time that he had. But that didn't prove anything.

Did it?

o o o

Fifteen years later and lying on his back in a motel room that needed a facelift, Nick woke to an image of Jesus Christ floating just above him in the air. He couldn't move or speak. His eyes seemed to be trying to jump from their sockets. His mouth formed a silent O, just as it did back in Avon on the day he thought he spotted his dad outside of Elko's garage.

What he saw was the classic, Biblical image of Christ — long hair, beard, flowing (red) robe, arms outstretched as if in welcoming. In his right hand, Jesus held a rose the color of blood. As Nick watched, the image simultaneously moved away from him and seemed to fade. It reached a point on the far wall and disappeared entirely.

Nick's heart hammered. His mind spun. *If you die in a dream, you die in real life,* Jack had told him. Was it possible?

Nick's mind immediately tried to assure him that the vison of Jesus was all part of the dream. He was still asleep and didn't wake up until after the apparition had faded.

He desperately wanted to believe it — would have given anything for it to be true. But as he sat up and tried to shake off the nightmare and the subsequent vision, he saw something lying near his bare left foot. Nick had only vague memories of much of the previous night (*loving you isn't the right thing to do*) but could not imagine what he could have been up to that would have resulted in him bringing the item into the room with him.

It was a rose petal.

o   o   o

Although he had not been suffering from panic attacks for very long, Nick was quickly coming to the realization that they were not only terrifying but also a crafty, calculating adversary. When they first cropped up, the attacks were focused on his throat: He felt as though his windpipe was closing up, and he couldn't breathe. But after surviving a few such episodes it became easier to work through them. *The last one didn't kill you and neither will this one,* he'd tell himself. *It's all in your mind. Your throat is fine.*

And so it was.

Not to be deterred, the panic changed tactics. *You are having a heart attack,* it told him. Those attacks not only forced him to continually check his pulse (which of course was at that point skyrocketing) it caused him to spend too much time thinking about the job of the heart. The muscle never, ever got a break once its work began at birth. Never. It had to keep beating minute after minute. Hour after hour, without end. It never got a day off.

It was a horrifying thought.

After surviving a few bouts of that ailment, Nick began to understand that, like his phantom throat issues, the heart problems too were all in his head.

That was followed by a period of "strokes" that led to Nick spelling "world" backward while checking his reflection in the bathroom mirror to see if his face was drooping. He had read somewhere that a sagging face and/or the inability to spell a simple word backward were sure signs of a stroke. After a few days of repeating "DLROW" the strokes dried up.

So the panic again changed course.

And the form that it took on that morning in Pocataw was the scariest, most devious yet.

Five years earlier — like much of the country — he had gone to witness William Friedkin's hellacious adaptation of William Peter Blatty's novel, The Exorcist. He had read the reports of people across the country fleeing from movie theaters in terror and could not resist seeing for himself what all the excitement was about. It was a huge mistake. He stayed to the end but left the theater shaken to his core.

The next morning, he walked into a church for the first time in years. He sat in one of the pews for a while and tried to soak in some of the peaceful atmosphere. He almost approached one of the priests to seek some comfort but chickened out in the end. Nick just couldn't bring himself to admit to being so rocked by a horror movie. But on the way out he dipped two fingers into the holy water font and blessed himself as he'd seen Father Damien Karras do in the film.

The combination of the time spent in the church and the self-blessing seemed to work.

After a couple of days, the movie's grip on him faded and was eventually forgotten. Until that Sunday morning in Pocataw.

CHAPTER ELEVEN

As the image of Christ faded, and Nick spotted the single rose petal on the ground, he first thought of Jack and his ominous warning. Could that be it? Was he so close to death that Christ had shown up to welcome him into the afterlife? The idea was preposterous but did not feel that way. Not at all. Nick was positive he had not dreamt the Jesus-image. And, even if he had, how could he explain the presence of the petal?

From there, his mind (surprisingly but only briefly) attempted to put a positive spin on the incident. If he actually did see the Son of God, it was proof of life after death and the promise of heaven. Wouldn't it be much easier to move through his remaining days knowing that there actually was a purpose and meaning behind it all?

Maybe.

But then the panic moved in, and all positive thoughts were lost in the ensuing red haze. *Forget all that nonsense,* it told him, *Christ did not appear to shepherd you into the afterlife or even to show you that such a plane exists. He was actually here, make no mistake about that. But He came to warn you. And, hey Nick, how much trouble must you be in for Jesus Christ himself to show up? Think about that for a second, buddy.*

Warn me about what? he thought, his pulse quickening.

But in an instant he knew.

Demons. Possession. Hell. Eternal damnation. And the biggie: Satan himself.

Nick scrambled up off the floor, his eyes wide, looking everywhere, seeing nothing. "God, Jesus, please help me in my time of need," he prayed aloud. It was something he had started doing during those few frightening days in the aftermath of watching The Exorcist. It seemed to help then, and it came back to him immediately. "God, Jesus, please help me in my time of need." He said it over as he tried to get control of himself.

He wanted so badly to bolt from the room, run down the stairwell and out into the sun. But he knew from prior experience that giving in to the panic was the worst thing he could do. He had to ride it out.

"God, Jesus, please help me in my time of need."

He would not allow himself to leave until he had the attack under control, but he could at least get some air. He forced himself to walk slowly over to the sliding glass door, pulled it back and went out onto the little balcony. He put both hands on the rusting, metal rail and tried to control his breathing.

Nick could feel himself calming, if only a little. His breathing was returning to normal and his heart rate was slowing (from a break-neck sprint to a fast run). He filled his lungs again and recited his prayer. It seemed to be working.

And then, unbidden, a foreign though filled his head. It came so suddenly and with such force that Nick thought someone had spoken it out loud.

You are going to jump. He yanked his hands from the railing as if they'd been burned and stumbled backward. His feet caught on the track for the sliding door and he fell on his butt. Nick scrambled to his feet and slammed the glass door hard enough that it shook in its metal frame. He stood there, breathing as if he'd run a marathon, and tried again to get himself under control.

What is happening?

During his brief time dealing with panic attacks, Nick had never experienced anything like that. The dream of the figure in the top hat (again) and waking to the image of Christ was already more than his overheated mind could handle. And then that voice with the ominous warning. It was panic overload.

Against his better judgement, he ran across the room (barefoot) and grabbed the door to the hallway. He was halfway out when he somehow stopped himself. No! He would not give in. Even if it meant that he would die or go mad or whatever the ultimate result would be, it was going to happen inside that shitty little room. He would not go running down the strip like a madman.

He re-entered the room and shut the door. One breathing exercise that he'd had some early success with involved taking a deep breath, holding it for three seconds (count them) and then breathing out slowly through his nose. He tried it then, waited a few seconds and repeated the process.

Maybe it was just his imagination, but Nick believed that his heart rate was slowing, at least to some degree. He sat down on the bed and continued trying to regulate his breathing.

He began to feel more in control but knew from experience that the panic episodes rarely ended with the first return to normal. The process almost always involved successively smaller panicked peaks and calmer valleys until it petered out altogether. He was feeling more like himself and thought maybe he would avoid the dragged-out recovery process for once when he started thinking about that voice at the railing.

Did he really think he was going to jump to his death against his will? How crazy was that? Nick got up off the bed and started toward the balcony. Part of him screamed out against the idea of going back out there. Nick was not familiar with the term exposure therapy but already understood on some level that if he didn't face the fear immediately it would linger and fester. He needed to confront it head on.

Nick opened the slider but at first remained safely inside the room, his feet on the edge of the aging blue carpet. He steadied himself and put one foot on the concrete balcony. The sounds of cars and tourists on the strip below gave him a sense of reassurance, and the right foot followed the left. Still well back from the railing, he bent forward and gripped the metal. Nothing happened. The voice in his head remained silent. Slowly, he shuffled his feet forward until he was standing flush with the rail.

He stood there and watched as a few of the Pocataw businesses started coming to life. Sundays were normally quiet as vacationers dealt with hangovers and prepared to head back home for the work week, but the next day was the holiday, so that particular Sunday would likely be an extension of the previous day's debauchery for many visitors.

Nick stayed outside just long enough to prove his point to himself and then went back into the room. He even smiled a little at how silly he had acted. He walked over to the ancient television and flipped it on. How could he have believed — even for a second — that he would suddenly and without reason jump from the balcony against his will? It was nuts.

He stopped.

Yes, it was crazy.

It was...it was the kind of thought that proved something was wrong with his brain. Normal people did not have thoughts like that, even for a fleeting moment. Therefore, something was not right with his head. Something had gone wrong inside his cranium while he slept. It made perfect sense. It explained the vision of Jesus hovering above his prone body. But what exactly had happened? Aneurism? Stroke? Brain bleed? The possibilities were endless. The panic spiral began once again.

o   o   o

An hour later, the cycle had played itself out, and an exhausted Nick Sampson checked out of room 404. He walked out to the strip. The sun was already blazing overhead. It was going to be a hot one.

On the way down in the elevator he had come to a decision. He was going to call Gina and tell her everything. The panic attacks, the dreams, the Jesus sighting, the episode at the railing. He would lay it all bare (except the meeting with Michelle) and pray that she could make sense of it. Nick immediately felt better.

The lone payphone in Pocataw was situated almost exactly at the strip's midpoint in front of the SportCenter Arcade. If it was being used by someone else, and you didn't want to wait, you had to trek down to the little campground at the western edge of the town to find another.

Nick crossed the street and headed to the phone. He picked up the handset and was ready to drop the two dimes when he heard a commotion in the arcade directly behind him. He hung up and looked inside. When the arcade was closed, a huge, white garage door covered the front of the building. Now it was rolled up, creating an open-air entrance on the entire front of the structure. Nick strolled inside among the flashing lights and electronic sounds of the pinball machines, video games and other attractions.

Among those, were games Nick always referred to simply as the "claw machines." The idea was to use the game's two knobs to guide a hanging claw (one moved it front to back, the other side to side) into position above the desired prize. For a quarter, the claw would drop and attempt to grab something from the pool of assorted "prizes" below.

A boy who must have been about eight or nine years old was pressed up against one of the machines and watched the claw grasp and then immediately drop what looked like a deck of playing cards.

"Shit!" the kid yelled. He had a black ball cap on backward, and apparently the machine had just claimed his quarter. He noticed Nick standing there and looked a little sheepish at having sworn in the presence of an adult.

"Tough break kid," Nick said. "I think that's too heavy. Try for something else." A sneaky little grin broke out on the kid's face. He reached into the back pocket of his jeans and pulled something out.

"You sure?" He flashed Nick a pack of the cards identical to the one the machine had just dropped. On the front of the box was a young woman wearing a bikini bottom but no top. The kid took a furtive glance around and quickly shoved the cards back into his pocket.

Nick realized it must have been the boy's roar of triumph at winning the cards that had attracted his attention while he was at the phone outside.

"One quarter left," the kid said. He carefully twisted the knob controlling the side-to-side movement a half turn, gazed into the glass case to check the claw's position and dropped the coin into the slot. The claw fell. Nick could tell immediately that the kid had overcompensated. The front of the claw banged off the deck of cards and fell into the smaller prizes scattered around it. Nick was ready to dig out a quarter of his own to give the boy another shot when he noticed the claw carrying something from the surface.

It was a necklace.

The kid looked crestfallen but reached into the prize slot and pulled it out. It was a cheap metal thing on an even cheaper silver chain. The pendant itself was painted white and was shaped like a bird. Nick thought it was supposed to be a seagull.

The thing was probably worth about five cents (or less), and the chain would undoubtedly turn the wearer's neck green, but there was something about it. Nick watched as the kid turned it over in his hands and then moved to shove it into his front pocket.

Nick stopped his hand.

"Kid, what's your name?" Nick asked.

"Mike," the boy replied. "Mike Turner."

"I'm Nick Sampson. Where you from, Mike?

"Brushton Mills. It's near Pittsburgh."

"That's where I'm from. Pittsburgh, I mean." Nick pulled out his wallet and grabbed a dollar bill. He held it out. "Can I buy that?"

Mike was looking for the joke. A dollar for that necklace? The guy had to be pulling his leg. "Uh, sure," he said. He grabbed the dollar, gave Nick the necklace and tore out of the arcade before Nick could change his mind.

Nick turned the necklace over in his hands. He wasn't interested in it because it depicted a seagull. It was the shape that captivated him. The bird's wings were spread at a 90-degree angle from the body, and the effect was that it looked like a mathematical plus sign.

Or a cross.

After everything that happened in the hotel room, Nick thought he could use all the divine help that he could get. He put the chain around his neck and walked back out to the payphone.

o   o   o

The conversation with Gina was brief. He gave her the highlights, but the incident with the kid from Pittsburgh left Nick feeling a little better, and he decided not to dump everything on Gina just yet. And not over the phone. He was still committed to telling her what was going on but thought it should be done face to face.

Nick wanted desperately to get home, but he had one more stop to make first. He crossed the strip and headed back to the state park where he had been writing when he met Michelle the day before. That whole meeting and subsequent "date" at the bar with her seemed like weeks before.

He passed the ball field and the large pavilion and walked down the sand-covered steps to the beach. The wind was up, and the waves were large enough to keep the few other visitors on the beach and out of the water. At the bottom of the steps, he turned left and walked about 100 yards to a spot where wind and time had carved a little shaded opening below the hillside that overlooked the sand and water.

It was right there that the photo of the four Sampson men had been snapped (by Ellen) in the summer of 1964. Because of the age difference, Nick had grown up without ever getting to know Nate or Nevin. Not like a brother should, anyway. His memories of both were spotty at best. But both of his brothers had been there, in that spot, 14 years earlier.

Nick stood there for a minute looking at the white sand and thinking about the mystery of the passage of time. In some ways he could see that distant moment, when the whole family was together, as if it had happened a week earlier. But, at the same time, Nate and Nevin often seemed like characters that he had only read about in a book.

They were simply fictions of some writer's imagination.

But on that hot day in the summer of 1964, they most definitely were real. Nick knew that because they may have saved his life.

Every family has stories that get repeated far more often than they deserve. These are the tales that get dragged out every Christmas morning, at every Thanksgiving dinner and often during family picnics. They typically begin with lines like "do you remember the time Nick almost drowned..."

CHAPTER TWELVE

No one was watching Nick.

*He was used to being the center of his parents'
attention because Nate was in the service and Nevin
was away at college. There was usually no one else for
them to focus on. But not on that day. Nevin was home
from school for the summer break and Nate had
shocked his parents (and Nevin and Nick) by taking a
leave and showing up unannounced in Pocataw.*

*The four older Sampsons sat on a pale yellow quilt and
sipped Cokes. There was so much to catch up on,
especially with Nate. Ed watched Ellen watching her
oldest son and thought she looked like a school girl
gazing at her first crush. She hung on his every word.*

*Nick, however, had little interest in Nate's stories of
life in the Marines. Not even his ominous warning
about the trouble brewing in Southeast Asia and his
own potential involvement there. Sure, Nick was
ecstatic to have both of his big brothers around for a
change. He just didn't like having to share the
spotlight. So he decided to do something about it.*

As the adults talked, Nick started throwing an orange rubber ball high into the summer sky and running under it to show his brothers his fielding skills.

"Nate, Nevin...watch!"

He reached down and fired the little ball high into the air. The wind was picking up and it caught the ball and blew it a few yards down the beach. Nick scampered to his left and arrived just in time to snag it with his left hand.

"You see that!?" he yelled.

"Nice one Nick," Nate said. "The Pirates could use you."

Nick beamed. Neither of his brothers were around to see his baseball or football games. At least one of his parents usually showed up but not always. And, even still, it wasn't the same as having one of his older brothers there. Especially Nate. Nick had grown up hearing stories galore of Nate's talent on the baseball field. To hear his mom tell it, the sky was the limit for a potential baseball career if he wouldn't have cut it short by joining the Marines at 18. A few college scouts had even sniffed around, but Nate had other plans.

Nick looked over again and saw the adults all laughing at something one of them had said. He reared back and fired the ball skyward as hard as he could. The throw knocked him off his feet for a second, but he popped up, brushed the sand off his butt and started following the arc of the ball. This time he had held on a second too long, and so the ball was headed out over the water. Damn. He didn't mind getting wet but there would be no time to wade in and gradually adjust to the lake's cold temps.

He held his breath and started high stepping away from the shore. He took a quick peek at the water then his eyes shot back into the sky to locate the ball. His mind made some quick calculations, and he realized he might be able to catch the ball, but it would be close. Four more quick splashing steps got him to within 10 feet of where the ball was going to land. Nick gulped air and leapt as far as he could. The ball ticked off his outstretched left hand and splashed into the water.

Damn it!

Nick spit out a mouthful of Lake Pocataw and immediately looked in to see if anyone had witnessed the drop. It didn't look like it. He was momentarily happy that no one was paying attention. He went to grab the ball for another round but couldn't spot it. It was a heavy rubber ball, and Nick assumed it would float. But that neon orange should have been easy to spot atop the clear water.

It was nowhere to be seen.

No great loss but it was the only ball they had brought to the beach, and Nick was hoping to talk at least one of his brothers into a game of catch at some point. He started walking back and forth in the water, looking both on the surface and below. The ball seemed to have disappeared. Two more steps from shore and the sand beneath his feet shifted sharply downward. Nick could no longer touch the bottom. He was a capable swimmer though and wasn't worried. He started doing a little doggy-paddle with his hands — just enough to keep himself afloat but not so much movement that would prevent him from seeing the sandy bottom.

And then he spotted the ball laying on the lakebed. "I can't believe it sank," he whispered to himself. Nick took a deep breath and headed down to grab the ball.

Although he spent a bit of time at the community pool each summer, Nick had never gotten comfortable opening his eyes under water. The chlorine burned.

So after feeling around blindly in the sand for a few seconds, he came up empty on his first dive. Nick resurfaced and took a few breaths while he paddled to stay afloat. He took another quick look in at his family, but no one seemed to be paying him any attention. He relocated the ball and submerged again. This time he went straight to it and grabbed the ball with his left hand. Gotcha, he thought. He quickly pivoted his body so that he could push off the bottom. But as he did, his left foot got tangled in something, and he could not shake free.

More annoyed than scared (at first, anyway) Nick propelled himself back down to see what was holding him. This time he did open his eyes, and he saw that his foot was tangled in some seaweed. He bent over and pulled and yanked on the vegetation while twisting his foot, but it wouldn't break loose.

It was then that the panic hit. Nick's eyes bulged and he expelled the last of his air. He clawed at the weeds with all his might. He was able to tear some of it away, but his foot remained stuck. His lungs burned and his body screamed for oxygen. It took all his willpower not to draw in a mouthful of lake water. Am I going to die? his confused and terrified mind wondered.

But unbeknownst to Nick, Nate had glanced up 30 seconds earlier and immediately noticed his little brother was nowhere in sight. A quick search left and right revealed a totally deserted beach. There was only one place Nick could be.

"Nevin, now!" he screamed and sprinted into the water.

Nevin at first had no idea what Nate was doing but heard the urgency in his brother's voice and bolted after him. Ed and Ellen sat stunned on the blanket, dumfounded.

The U.S. Marines pride themselves on being an amphibious fighting force, and Nate spent a week in the pool at Parris Island during boot camp being subjected to every water-based test his humorless drill instructors could think up. He spent hours in the water not only wearing a full combat uniform and boots but often carrying a 50-pound pack too.

So despite being fully dressed, he hit the water like a missile and spotted Nick struggling just below the surface seconds later. He dove at Nick's legs and quickly ripped his foot free. Nate grabbed Nick around the torso with his left hand and swam to the surface with his right.

Nick broke the surface of the water and pulled in a huge gulp of air. And then another. His rescue had occurred so quickly he wasn't even sure what *happened. He looked around and saw Nevin standing nearby looking shaken. He realized Nate was still holding him.*

Nate seemed unfazed. In fact, he was smiling.

"Were you looking for this, little brother?"

In the hand that wasn't still holding onto Nick, Nate had the orange ball.

o o o

An hour later, the seriousness of the situation was already fading, and Nick was enduring some ribbing from his brothers, and even a little from his parents. His dad told him the next time something like that happened there might not be a Marine around to save him.

"Your mom wouldn't get her hair wet no matter what, Nick, so you gotta be careful." At that, Ellen swatted Ed lightly on the arm, and the family all had a laugh.

Ellen said it was just about dinner time and that they should get going back to the cabin. She started gathering the family's belongings into the wicker baskets they had brought to the beach.

"Hang on," Ed said. "We need to preserve this on film. It's not every day that one of my sons saves another

from certain death." There were chuckles all around as he reached into one of the baskets and pulled out Ellen's Nikon. She immediately took it from him.

"No way I'm getting in this picture," she said. "I'm a mess. Get over there with your boys."

The Sampson men lined up side by side, but Ed told Nick to get in front of him. "I want you here where I can keep an eye on you," he joked. Nick did as he was told. As Nevin and Nate flanked him, Ed put his hands on Nick's shoulders. "Say cheese everyone," Ellen said. She brought the camera to her eye and pressed the shutter.

o   o   o

Nick Sampson was born in 1953 while the war in Korea was coming to a close. In 1972, the year he turned 19, he received a notice from the U.S. Government that he was eligible for the military draft slated to be held the next year.

This news did not fill Nick with joy.

He had already lost one brother to the ongoing war in Vietnam and had another brother who, for some reason, was chomping at the bit to pack up his camera and get over there for a better look.

Nick was fine staying behind in Avon, thank you very much.

It sounded like his country had other plans. In February of 1972, a drawing was held to determine draft priority numbers for men, like Nick, who were born in 1953.

But then the skies cleared.

In January of 1973, the government announced that no further draft orders would be issued. To say that news came as a relief for Nick Sampson would be a monumental understatement. He saw the story while he and his mom were watching the 6 o'clock news one night on KDKA. He would never have admitted it, but he had been unable to think of much other than Vietnam after receiving the notification the year before. He had briefly considered fleeing north to Canada like so many others seemed to be doing, but it was never a serious option.

It would have been a slap in the face to Nate's memory.

Nick and his mom hugged briefly after the news broke, and they both wiped away a few tears.

Nick had no doubt her thoughts were at least partially of Nate. Nick's were too.

At that point in his life (and continuing into 1978) receiving any bit of good news, no matter how small, was an impetus to celebrate. And Nick knew only one way to do that.

He got drunk for two days.

But he eventually had to sober up, and with that came the realization that he had no real plans for his future. He had been working at Kingston since he graduated from high school the year before, but it felt like a placeholder until the situation in Vietnam played itself out. Nick found that it was impossible to try to plan anything with the war and his possible deployment there hanging over his head.

And there was also the fact that Nick had hated school, and the thought of adding more of it by going to college sounded awful. On top of that, he had little interest in learning a trade like carpentry or plumbing. So what options did that leave, exactly?

Nick had no clue. The Vietnam situation had afforded him the opportunity to bury that whole line of thinking for a while. But then, on that day in February of 1972, it was suddenly starring him directly in the face.

o   o   o

The Tuesday after the Memorial Day weekend, Nick reported to work (after dropping off some items in the nest) and was immediately notified that he would not be manning the slitter that day. It was not unusual — for a variety of reasons — for Kingston's workers to shuffle around from work station to work station on any given day. And while none of the positions were much better or worse than any other, the one semi-cushy job was the mixer.

On the second floor of the plant, overlooking the work floor, a large room held the two enormous stainless-steel vats in which the soda was mixed and prepared to be bottled down below.

Heavy-duty rubber pipes carried the two main ingredients needed to make the soft drinks to the holding tanks: water and sugar. So the person in charge of mixing only needed to add the coloring, the flavoring and a chemical — sodium benzoate

— that prevented mold from forming in the "pop."

Those ingredients arrived at the Kingston plant in 20-gallon buckets, and the mixer was responsible for getting them up the small metal ladder and dumping them into the vats with the sugar and water. It was hard work but only had to be done a few times a day, depending on production levels.

On most days, Kingston's mixer was one Don Calhoun, who had seniority over everyone in the plant except Bill Morton. Morton could have claimed the mixer job but didn't like the idea of being all alone up in the building's rafters all day. At his workstation, he could at least occasionally shoot the shit with his co-workers.

But the isolation didn't bother Calhoun, who was known as "haystacks" to his co-wasworkers. Because like the famous studio wrester of the same surname, Don weighed 500 pounds if he weighed an ounce.

"Haystacks called off sick today," Mark DeFazio told Nick as soon as he punched in for the day. "I want you mixing."

"He's probably busy with that PlayGirl centerfold shoot. That guy is one gorgeous hunk of man."

DeFazio starred at Nick for a beat and then walked away.

DeFazio's father, Dean, owned the plant. And Mark was Freddy Baxter's boss and, maybe more importantly, served as a buffer between his dad and the rest of the workers.

The old man's temper was legendary.

A day as the mixer was a blessing, and Nick wasted no time getting upstairs. He briefly wondered if he could run out to the nest to grab a couple beers for the morning. As mixer, he would almost certainly have zero interaction with anyone else.

Oh well, they'll still be there at lunchtime, he thought.

When he got upstairs, Nick saw that the primary tank was full of creamy cherry and was ready to go. Freddy would press a buzzer when everything was set downstairs, and Nick would only need to flip a switch to start the soda on its journey.

"Today's gonna be a picnic," Nick told the empty chamber.

o   o   o

About halfway through the morning, right after Nick prepared tank 2 with the pina colada that would be bottled in the afternoon, he realized he had a couple of free hours (assuming there were no problems). He grabbed a pencil and a scrap of paper off the little table in the corner that Haystacks used as a desk. He was pretty sure he knew where he left off his "Peter" story, which was hidden under his bed at home.

He bit on the eraser end of the pencil for a few moments and then put the lead to the paper. He wrote:

I should tell you what I meant before about his drinking. It is most definitely a major contributor to his state of depression. Peter drinks every weekend. There are no exceptions. Every Friday Peter gets his mom to drive him to the local beer distributor and he buys a case of beer. Again, this might sound harmless until you realize that I mean EVERY. SINGLE. WEEKEND. No matter what. One year, he was so sick with the flu he could barely get out of bed. But there on the nightstand beside the bed sat a tall can of Pabst. It was right next to the Kleenex. I sometimes wonder what would happen if his mom died on a Saturday. Would he skip drinking that weekend? No way. I think it's more likely that he would curse his mom for the bad timing. And then he would attend the funeral, sure, but I promise you he'd have a fucking beer tucked into his fucking suit pocket.

CHAPTER THIRTEEN

Tuesdays were typically an off day for Gina because she worked most Saturdays and Sundays. When Nick emerged from the Kingston plant later that day Gina was standing outside, waiting.

Nick was ready to start the ruse of heading home before turning back to the nest to grab the empties from that day's lunch when he spotted Gina.

"Can I help you ma'am?" he said. "We don't actually sell the pop here if that's what you need. You'll have to go to the A&P."

"Good one."

Nick noticed Gina was wearing a top he'd never seen before. It was a dark blue with bright orange specks splattered across the front. It looked like someone had flicked a paintbrush at her.

"Nice shirt," he said. "So what brings you here?"

"I need to go the bakery and thought maybe you could join me. I want to hear more of what you were saying on the phone over the weekend." The anxiety. The panic. The dreams.

He didn't want to get into it but knew that it would help to talk to someone about what was happening. Nick supposed that day was as good a time as any.

"Ok sure. But I gotta get something first." He shot a glance toward the nest.

"Leave it," she said. "We're going the other direction. You can get them on the way back home, and I don't think you want to take your beer into the bakery." She glanced him up and down. "By the way, you smell like a brewery." Nick shrugged.

They turned and headed away from Nick's house and toward Fred's Bakery. The last of the Kingston workers were driving out of the little parking lot.

Cars sped by on Woodstock Street as the two headed deeper into the commercial and industrial part of Avon. Loud music blared from the open windows of many of them. Nick thought part of Gina's reasoning for wanting him to tag along was that she didn't feel especially safe walking down there alone.

He didn't blame her.

"So you said something on the phone about a rose?" Gina said. "How did that play into the dreams?"

Nick told her about his vision of Jesus holding the rose and how he subsequently found a rose petal laying near his foot.

Gina at first didn't respond. She remained quiet for so long that Nick was about to ask if she'd heard him.

"Bear with me here, Nick, and don't get upset. I'm just trying to look at this logically," she looked over but he kept his gaze straight ahead, noncommittal. "What if we come at this the opposite way?"

Then he did look at her. "What do you mean?"

"Well, instead of assuming you saw the vision and then saw the rose petal, what if it happened the other way? You said yourself that you were pretty drunk when you got back to the room the night before. What if you subconsciously noticed the petal late that night, and then your mind went to work and conjured up the rose in His hand while you were asleep? Maybe the cleaning woman just missed it after the last guest checked out."

Nick had wondered if he had somehow dragged the petal into the room himself as soon as he saw it. He had not considered that it might have already been there.

Gina's explanation made perfect sense and was certainly more likely than what Nick believed had happened. But he wasn't buying it. He told her that.

"It just doesn't feel right," he said. "I know how crazy this sounds, but I'm positive it wasn't there the night before. I know it."

"Not that it would prove anything, but I wish you would have brought it with you," Gina said.

She looked over and saw a sly smile cross Nick's face.

"You did?"

They were approaching the bridge where Woodstock Street crossed over the railroad tracks.

Just before the bridge, the land sloped off sharply on the right, ending at the railroad tracks and the creek below.

Just as Nick reached for the wallet in his back pocket, two of Avon's homeless appeared from the drop off on Gina's right.

"Hey lady, you got a quarter?" one of them asked. Nick could smell the guy as well as he could see him. The stench was a combination of cheap wine and Sterno, he thought.

"Just keep moving," Nick told Gina.

Nick looked in the direction the men had come from and could see a makeshift tent erected among the trees and shrubs near the creek. There was debris scattered all around the outside.

"Jesus," he whispered to Gina. "Do they live in that?"

She didn't respond but took a quick peek over her shoulder to make sure the panhandlers were not following. They had disappeared.

Living outside in the spring and summer was one thing, but what about when it got cold? Or rained?

And where did one go to the bathroom? Nick wondered as they crossed the bridge.

"What do you mean, Nick?" Gina said. "They basically just took your nest idea to the next level."

o   o   o

Fred's Bakery was an Avon icon.

Along with the "Brigantine" sub sandwich created and sold by the Triangle Bar on the other side of town, the pastries and freshly-baked bread from Fred's probably brought more people into the borough than anything else.

They mystery was why the bakery had never relocated to a better spot. It was buried among various warehouses, industrial operations and junk yards. The town dump was not far away either.

But everyone knew where Fred's was, and the location didn't seem to stop customers from visiting.

Nick walked in behind Gina and was immediately hit by the sweet smell of donuts, crescent rolls, cakes and other assorted goodies.

He thought to himself that you probably gained a pound just walking through the door.

"This is probably what heaven smells like," he said.

When Nick was a boy, his dad would often run down to the bakery on Saturday mornings and bring back a white sack full of sweets for breakfast and a large coffee for himself. Occasionally, Nick would tag along. He especially liked to watch the noisy old bread slicer in action. There was no lunch as good as a thick piece of Fred's fresh bread slathered with peanut butter, in Nick Sampson's humble opinion.

Gina paid for her purchases, and she and Nick walked out. They started back toward the Kingston plant (and the nest) and their homes beyond.

"You didn't finish what you were saying about the rose petal before those homeless guys showed up," Gina said. "Did you take the petal with you?"

Before leaving the Poolside Motel, Nick picked the rose petal off the floor. He had no luggage in which to put it, so he opened his wallet and carefully placed it in one of the little plastic windows designed to hold photos. There were no pictures in the wallet.

As he and Gina walked home, Nick stopped, pulled out his wallet and opened it up.

A perplexed look crossed his face, and he glanced over at Gina. She knew without asking.

The rose petal was gone.

o o o

The one-year anniversary of Nate's death fell two days after Easter in 1966.

Nick came home from school and was a little surprise to see Ed there. His dad was working the three-to-eleven shift at the mill and usually left just before Nick got off the school bus. Nick also noticed that his mother wasn't in her customary spot on the couch.

"Where's mom?"

"She had to run to the A&P. She won't be long."

"And why are you still here? Won't you be late?"

Punctuality rated right up there with God, country and the Pittsburgh Steelers in the Ed Sampson pantheon of values. He was never late for anything.

"Let's take a walk," Ed said.

He led Nick along Waverly Street (in the opposite direction of the Kingston plant where Nick would be working in a few years) and climbed over the guardrail and onto the embankment above the railroad tracks. A path had been worn through the brush there and was used often by people who needed to get across town but didn't want to walk the whole way over to the Washington Street bridge.

They both instinctively looked for trains before crossing the tracks, although it was more habit than anything else. You could hear those trains coming from a mile away. They didn't sneak up on anyone.

"Where we going?" Nick asked when they stepped across the last rail.

"Right here." His dad pointed to a pink, concrete building that stood in the center of a small parking lot just on the other side of the tracks. The Very Dairy. The town's milk store sold, well basically just milk and other dairy products, although it also stocked the baseball trading cards that Nick collected religiously.

As they got closer, it occurred to Nick that the milk store was one of at least three businesses in Avon that had the word "dairy" in their names. There was also the Dairy Delite and the Village Dairy. The latter sat near Elko's Garage and served as a combo café, deli and general store. Nick had consumed more than his share of chocolate malteds while sitting on one of the circular, red-leather stools at the Village Dairy counter.

"You said mom was at the store. Won't she get milk?"

"We're not getting milk," Ed replied.

They walked over to one of the freezers, and Ed withdrew two ice cream sandwiches — chocolate for Nick and strawberry for himself. He paid and they walked out. There was a small bench located on one side of the store, and Ed gestured for Nick to sit.

"Thanks dad," Nick said.

His dad didn't respond but instead watched the pedestrian and vehicle traffic on Noble Street. They sat quietly and worked on the ice cream treats. A couple of minutes later, a man in a tattered overcoat stumbled down the opposite side of the street. Nick thought it would be a miracle if the guy didn't fall, and soon. He didn't really know what "drunk" was but suspected he might be looking at it.

Ed shook his head.

"Reminds me of my old man," he said. "Never met a saloon he didn't like." He seemed to be talking more to himself than his son. Ed turned and looked at Nick. "I ever tell you about your grandfather?"

They both knew that Ed hardly ever spoke of his dad. It was made clear to Nick and his brothers at an early age that the topic was off limits.

"Not much."

"He was the town drunk. Sort of like Brownie except for one thing. He was a great dresser. I know that makes no sense, but there you have it." He took the last bite of the ice cream.

"He would be stumbling all over town, pissing all over himself, but he was always dressed to the nines. And he never went out of the house without that stupid hat."

"Like a baseball cap?"

Ed Sampson chuckled.

"No Nick. A top hat."

Nick remembered one of the few photos he had ever seen of his dad as a kid. In it, a 10 or 11-year-old Eddie stood on a sidewalk in front of a formally-dressed man and woman who were undoubtedly his parents. A top hat sat crookedly on the man's head.

They were both finished with the ice cream, and Nick figured his dad would be ready to head back home, but he just sat there. It wasn't at all like his dad to take Nick out just for the hell of it. Nick was starting to feel uneasy.

Ed balled up the paper wrapper his ice cream sandwich came in and took Nick's too. He walked over to a trash can that sat on the other side of the store and deposited them. When he sat back down and looked over, Nick was sure something was wrong. None of the little outing made any sense.

"One other thing I need to tell you, Nick." He looked down at his shoes. "Your mom loves you very much. And she loved Nevin very much."

Oh my God mom is dying, Nick thought. That's why we're here. The ice cream was supposed to help ease the pain.

"Never forget that and never doubt it. But there is a special bond between a woman and her first born. It's unique. When Nate died, the person your mom had been all her life died too. I don't know how to explain it any better. They say life goes on, and it does, but what *they don't tell you is that you are left with a huge hole that can never be filled and that will never disappear. Never." He looked up and Nick saw tears ready to spill down his unshaven cheeks. He wasn't sure he had ever seen his dad cry — not even on the day the Marines showed up with the news about Nate.*

Ed tried to compose himself.

There's more, Nick thought. Oh God what else is he going to tell me?

"It's important that you remember that. Can you do that?" Nick was too shaken to speak so he just nodded.

"Ok, good. That's good," Ed said. "And one more thing." He put his hand on the back of Nick's neck. "Nick I..." He took a deep breath and looked over at his youngest son.

"I think we should head home now."

o   o   o

Later that night, after Nick talked to his mom about his dad's departure (she would not admit it was permanent and kept insisting everything would be ok), Nick quietly cried himself to sleep.

And dreamed.

He was at one of his dad's softball games. Nick was sitting in the bleachers with his mom. He was drinking a Pepsi. His dad came to the plate, and Nick somehow knew it was the at-bat in which Ed would end up at third base with a broken foot. "Careful dad!" He tried to scream, but nothing came out.

Ed Sampson smashed the second pitch over the left fielder's head and trudged around the diamond. As he passed second base, Nick screamed at him to stay on his feet. "Don't slide!" He yelled. But the words either didn't materialize or his dad never heard them.

He slid into third just ahead of the throw, and kicked an enormous cloud of dirt and dust into the air.

Nicked looked on horrified, hoping his dad had somehow escaped the injury this time around.

But when the dust settled, things were even worse than he had feared.

His dad had disappeared.

CHAPTER FOURTEEN

Life went on pretty much as usual for Nick and Gina through the summer and early fall of 1978. They both continued working jobs they didn't much care for, and each remained a shoulder the other could lean on when life got especially tough.

Their lives stayed as predictable and bland as the pizza they occasionally ordered from Ventris' Pizzeria late on Saturday nights when nothing else was open.

Predictable and bland. Except for two incidents that involved the police.

The first cost Nick a night in jail.

The second took place in the nest and changed their lives forever.

o o o

On the 4th of July, Nick and his friend Marty Hawranko decided to drive 60 miles south to the horse racing track in Washington County. Marty worked at Kingston Bottling too, and the plant was closed for the holiday. Marty was a nice enough guy, but it wasn't his personality that led

Nick to think of him when the idea of a day at the track sprung to mind. No, Marty had one unique trait that made him the perfect partner for such an outing.

He didn't drink.

Marty picked Nick up at home in his new Dodge Aspen late that afternoon. He was unmarried and unattached, and so the car received not only all of Marty's attention but a big portion of his paycheck.

"Hey, watch the door," he told Nick as he climbed in. "And what is that?" He pointed to the brown paper bag Nick had on his lap.

Nick reached in and pulled out a six pack of 16-ounce Stroh's Beer.

"You know, they have beer at the track," Marty said.

"I know."

An hour later Marty gently pulled into the track's gravel lot and paid $5 to park. Marty thought the price was a little steep, but the flip side was that there was no fee to enter the track itself. Five bucks bought you parking and entry.

"Try to get as close as you can," Nick told him.

"What's the difference? You can't walk a little?" Marty replied. "I'd actually rather keep it near the back where it's less likely that someone pulls in close and dings the door." Nick said nothing.

Marty found a spot along the outer edges of the lot and killed the engine. Nick didn't say anything but sighed, shook his head and got out. He left the bag with the beer in the footwell.

The primary difference between thoroughbred racing and harness racing, which is what Nick and Marty would be watching (and betting on!), was that the "jockey" sat in a 2wheeled sulky attached to the horse by harnesses rather than riding on its back.

The speeds were much slower than in thoroughbred racing too, but Nick thought the little carts added a nice visual element for the spectators that thoroughbred racing lacked.

There was a building adjacent to the track itself that housed the betting windows, bathrooms and some food (and beer) stands. Just minutes before the first race, Nick walked inside and bet a $5 trifecta on three horses he had never heard of.

One of them was simply named "Suds" and he liked that. It was a long-shot, but the bet would pay at least $175 if all three horses finished in the right order.

"Go big or go home," Nick told Vora Testick, the window attendant who swapped his crumpled cash for a pink ticket (he read her name on the gold tag above her left breast). She didn't reply.

Nick walked back out to the track and found Marty along the rail near the finish line.

"Did you bet?" Nick asked.

'Nah."

"There's no racing without betting Marty. What fun is that? You're just watching a bunch of horses running in a circle." Marty shrugged.

The starting bell blared, and the horses began tearing for the first corner. People all around Nick and Marty started screaming, urging their horses on. Nick looked at his ticket to double check the numbers of his horses and then gazed out onto the track.

It wasn't going well.

Because of the distance, Nick had a hard time distinguishing one horse from another as they hit the far turn, but he thought his three were near the rear.

When the horses crossed the finish line half a minute later, Nick could not believe his eyes.

His horses did not only not come in first, second and third as they needed to for Nick to win his bet, but they were the last three across the line.

Marty laughed. "Oh man, you should win something for that Nick. It can't be easy to pick the three worst."

Nick threw his ticket on the ground.

"I'll be back in a minute. Can I have your keys?"

Marty had allowed no one — not even his dad — to drive the Aspen since he bought it two months earlier. It was his baby.

"What? Are you crazy? Why?" And then it clicked. The beer.

"Oh, hey, I thought you brought those for the ride home. I'll buy you a beer if you want, Nick."

It wasn't about the money (although Nick would take Marty up on his offer) but Nick would not be able to drink the way he wanted at the concession stand. He couldn't tell Marty that though.

"I don't like the brands they stock here. Don't worry, I won't do anything to your car. I'll be right back." He held out his hand.

Marty looked at him for a moment and then reached into his pocket and pulled out the keys. Without a word, he handed them over.

Nick broke into a trot and headed toward the lot, cursing Marty the whole way for parking so far from the entrance.

God, I'm in bad shape, he thought.

He finally reached the Aspen and climbed inside. He reached into the bag and withdrew one of the beers.

"Fuck you Suds," he said and drank.

o o o

That pattern went on through the evening — race, run to the car, chug — and Marty was growing increasingly worried. Worried about Nick's deteriorating condition and worried about his car.

He knew Nick had been complementing his own stash with beers at the concession stand, and he himself had bought two others for Nick. He had no idea how many drinks Nick had, but it was clearly too many. Marty was ready to get home. "Ready to call it a night Nick?" Marty asked after the eighth race. He expected some pushback but got none. But that had nothing to do with Nick's desire to win back some of his losses or because he was having a good time.

He was out of beer.

"Yep, let's go," Nick said. "You want to drive or should I?"

o o o

An hour later, Marty pulled up in front of the Sampson house, but Nick didn't want to get out. He asked Marty to take him to the Revco instead.

"I want to see if Gina's working."

"It's closed Nick. Fourth of July, remember?"

Nick just sat there. Marty desperately wanted him out of the car before, well, before he did something in the car that was going to need cleaned up. If taking him to the Revco would do the trick then that's what he would do.

Marty put the car in drive and pulled into the pharmacy's empty parking lot two minutes later. The store was completely dark.

"Here ya go Nick. Tell Gina I said hi."

Nick fumbled with the door handle but eventually figured it out. He staggered out into the night, and Marty quickly pulled away. It was the last social outing the two would ever take together. Nick lurched over to the store's front door and yanked on the handle. It did not budge. He tried again with no luck. Confused, he took a step back, lifted his right foot and drove it through the door's glass. He slipped and fell on his back with the bottom half of his leg sticking through the broken door's lower panel. An alarm began to sound inside the building.

Nick didn't hear it though. He was passed out.

Five minutes later, a police car pulled into the lot. Officer Murdoch quickly recognized Nick from his escapades at the McDonalds a few months earlier.

"No ride home tonight, pal," he said as he pulled out his handcuffs. "This time you stay with us."

o   o   o

Four months later, in early November, Nick was working the slitter one Wednesday morning when Dean Defazio, Kingston's owner, walked over.

Any visit from the old man was bad news. He never stopped by just to say hi. Nick could see Bill Morton at the head of the production line and knew he'd be dying to know what the old Italian wanted.

"Come with me," he said. Nick stayed close behind as DeFazio wound through the plant, and the two men were garnering looks from each worker they passed. The curiosity would be killing them.

Nick followed Mr. DeFazio outside and immediately knew he was in trouble. To his left, two police cars sat along Waverly Street with their light bars flashing. The cars were positioned directly in front of the nest.

Nick's heartbeat skyrocketed as he walked behind DeFazio over to where a small cluster of cops was standing. As the two men approached, the officers stopped talking. It was clear they were waiting for Nick.

Relax, he told himself. *There's no way they can connect you to this place. And even if they could, so what? A six pack of beer and a peanut butter sandwich is not against the law.*

As he walked, Nick let out a nervous little laugh. What was he so worried about? He hadn't even had any beer (yet) that day. He was thinking like a criminal, but he hadn't done anything wrong.

But still...something didn't feel right.

"This is Nick," DeFazio said to cops. At that, he turned and headed back to the plant.

Nick was doing his best to look the part of busy guy irritated by the interruption to his day. He didn't think he was pulling it off.

"Are you Nick Sampson?" one of the cops asked? He moved toward Nick.

"Yeah, that's me."

"I'm officer Burrows. What do you know about this spot?" He turned and gestured toward the embankment below the road. The nest was directly on the other side of the shrubs and bushes but it wasn't visible from where they were standing.

"Huh? Nothing. What do you mean?" Nick said.

Burrows looked at Nick. "There's a little clearing on the other side. We have reason to believe you've spent some time in there."

Sweat was pouring down the small of Nick's back. He struggled to breathe but tried not to show it. Part of his mind kept insisting he had done nothing wrong. None of it made any sense.

"No, I don't think so," Nick whispered. "And even if I did, so what? Is that a crime?" He was trying to put some bravado that he didn't feel into his words.

Burrows looked at the other cops and one nodded.

"We found something in here," Burrows said. "We thought you might be able to help us." Nick assumed it was his lunch.

Sure, Nick thought, *beers all around. Save one for me. They're mine after all.*

"What was it?" Nick asked. He suddenly knew the answer was not going to be beer or a sandwich.

Burrows starred him straight in the eyes.

"A body."

He watched Nick's reaction closely.

Nick was simultaneously horrified and relieved. He had nothing to do with whatever had happened in the nest, but at the same time it was his private spot. His mind whirled.

"That's terrible, but I can't help you," Nick said. "As I said, I've never been down there." With that, he turned and started back toward the bottling plant.

But he was not surprised when Burrows called his name after he took just a few steps. Nick turned and saw Burrows take something from one of the other officers.

It was a photograph sealed in a baggie.

"Then maybe you can explain this," Burrows said

Part Three

The

Homecoming

CHAPTER FIFTEEN

Ellen Sampson was born Ellen Marie Smith in 1913, five years after her husband was born. She was 16 when the Great Depression began, but her family was not as hard hit as many others. Her father, Carl, worked at a local glass manufacturer, and the plant never slowed down, even as the U.S. and local economies came to a virtual standstill.

The company made glass safety and signal lenses that were used by the railroad industry, and even as 15 million Americans lost their jobs, those railcars kept rolling on down the tracks.

Ellen never went hungry, but she had a good view of what real hunger looked like as she watched some of her Avon friends and neighbors. So good, in fact, that she vowed none of her own kids would ever want for anything.

That fact that she was only 16 didn't stop her from having such thoughts. She assumed she would eventually marry and have children, of course.

Everyone did.

The Sampsons scraped by on only Ed's pay from the mill for the first 30 years of their marriage, but when Nick turned 10 and was deemed old enough to be home alone after school, Ellen went looking for some supplemental income.

And she found it right across town.

At the end of a block of Noble Street that also housed the bowling alley and the record store, there was a small warehouse operated by the Spiegel Company. Like its mailorder competitors including Sears and Montgomery Ward, Speigel was a catalog–based retailer that sold everything from blenders and toasters to toys and guns.

The operation in Avon was mainly tasked with accepting returns but also kept some merchandise on hand and handled the billing for the company's eastern region, which included Pennsylvania, Ohio and West Virginia.

Ellen took a part-time job that entailed handling phone calls, dealing with walk-in customers who were making returns and basically anything else that needed done. She worked 20 hours a week and was paid $3.15 an hour.

For 11 months of the year the job was as hum drum as retail work could be. But in December — and especially in the two weeks right before Christmas — the place was a madhouse.

Seven days before Christmas in 1964, a truck delivering merchandise for the Avon operation arrived in the dirty little alley behind the store. It was full of clothes and coats and boots and — probably more than anything — toys that would soon sit wrapped beneath Christmas trees in Avon homes.

But the truck also held a heavy wooden crate full of hand tools.

The truck was quickly unloaded, and the "girls" who worked there were called to the back to begin opening boxes and organizing the contents on large metal shelves out of the view of the walk-in customers. Mr. Pierce, the store supervisor, first assigned Ellen to deal with a box full of toys that would be picked up by customers in the next few days.

But it was stuck behind the crate containing hammers and screwdrivers and wrenches. Rather than waste time asking for help, she tried to move the box herself.

She quickly regretted that decision.

As she bent and tried to lift the crate, Ellen felt something in her back give way. She knew immediately that it was bad. She called for Mr. Pierce, and he quickly (and gingerly) guided her into his car and drove her across town to see Dr. Brougher.

Brougher (gingerly) poked and prodded at her back and eventually told her that nothing seemed to be out of place, but spines were tricky, and the best thing she could do was to stay off her feet for a few days and get some rest.

He prescribed her some pain killers that he doubted she would need but "just in case you do."

Ellen quickly found that she did, in fact, need the pills. After Nate died the next year, she needed them even more. And in 1978, 14 years after she was injured, she was still taking the meds every day.

She never went back to Spiegel.

o o o

At about the same time Nick found out there had
been a visitor to his nest, Ellen was upstairs in her
bedroom. She had just taken the first of her three-
times-a-day medication. She did not sleep in the
room but visited it often. It was there that she
kept her small photo collection of her boys in a
shoebox under the bed.

The meds often made her feel melancholy, and
that often resulted in Ellen pulling out the old
pictures. There were not many (and Nick had
swiped the one now in the possession of the
police years before). She would spend a bit of
time gazing at yellowing photos of Nevin and
Nick in long-ago Halloween costumes or some in
which the younger boys were just sitting in the
front yard of the old house. But the one she came
back to (much) more often was Nate's official
Marine photo from Parris Island. In it, the young,
baby-faced soldier was sporting the same, ultra-
serious expression that all Marines seemingly
wore in those graduation pictures. There were
never any smiles, and Nate's was no different. He
wore the traditional white dress hat and the

"dress blues," although only the top of the coat was visible in the photo.

Ellen ran her finger over the old picture as the tears came on, as they often did.

She sat there for a long time.

o o o

Badly shaken, Nick returned to the slitter. His mind kept going off in a million different directions. How did anyone find the nest? Who was the guy? Was it even a "guy?" Burrows only said body, so theoretically it could have been a woman. How did they even know the kid in the picture was Nick? In his panic, it didn't even occur to him to deny it. And, most importantly, what did it all mean for his continued employment at Kingston?

He finished his shift and wanted to get home, down a dozen beers (he'd been cheated out of his lunchtime trip to the nest, after all, and assumed he'd never see those beers again) and forget the whole thing. As he stuck his timecard into the clock, Mr. DeFazio appeared from around the corner.

"Can you come in here for a minute, Nick?"

"Sure," he said, and followed the old man into his little office.

Nick sat down opposite the big leather chair on the far side of the desk and looked around. He'd only been in there once or twice since he got hired seven years ago. And on that day he wasn't in there long. There were no vague questions from some HR person about where he saw himself in five years. Hell, there was no HR person. Kingston needed able bodies, and Nick was a strong young guy. Enough said.

DeFazio kept a photo of his family in a gold frame on the desk. There were two other children, both younger than Mark. Nick had seen them around the plant from time to time but neither worked there yet. A victory for them, Nick thought.

On the rear wall, behind the desk, there was a framed collage containing labels of the 11 flavors that Kingson produced. Nick noticed the mint ginger ale label and realized they had not bottled that flavor for months, maybe longer. He'd actually forgotten about it. Beneath the frame was a gold plaque with the company's logo (a smiling

King with tilted crown) and slogan: "Beverage of the 'burgh."

DeFazio was normally not the type to waste time with pleasantries, and that day was no different.

"First of all, I'm the one who ID'd you in the photo, Nick. In case you were wondering. One of our drivers spotted the body from the cab of his truck and let me know. I took a look and called the cops." He paused, waited for Nick to respond, and when he didn't DeFazio continued.

"One look at that photo and I knew who it was. You haven't changed much."

Nick remembered thinking the nest was invisible on that side of the embankment but had never considered that a higher vantage point might change that. He didn't want to admit to anything, but hell, the photo was already out in the open and he was sure they found his lunch too. One question was nagging him.

"That picture was hidden. I don't understand how they even found it." "My understanding is the guy had it in his hand," DeFazio said.

That response answered one of Nick's questions – the body belonged to a man. *But how in the hell would he stumble on that photo? Heck, you could sit in that spot for a*

week and never find it, he thought.

Nick kept his poker face in place. He was giving away nothing.

"Next thing, the cops said there was a sandwich and a six-pack in there. You know anything about that?

The phrase *you have the right to remain silent* ran through Nick's mind. He shook his head?

"Nick, I really don't want to play games. Have you been drinking over there at lunch?"

Nick shifted in his seat. "No," he said. "But even if I did, I can do whatever I want on my own time. I'm off the clock. I wouldn't be the first guy who had a liquid lunch."

DeFazio reached down and picked up a pen laying on the blotter. He wrote something on a little notepad, but Nick couldn't read it from his vantage point.

"That's true, but we can't have guys working here drunk. Too dangerous with all this machinery." he paused. "Have you ever drank here in the plant?" To tell the truth and say yes would likely result in Nick losing his job.

"Nope," he said.

DeFazio frowned and reached into the bottom drawer of his desk. He pulled out a crushed Stroh's can.

"I found this in the trash next to the slitter a few weeks ago. Don't suppose you know anything about it, right?"

o   o   o

When he walked out of the plant and turned toward home, Nick immediately noticed the yellow police tape strung around the area where the body had been found. He wanted to tear it down and climb into the nest. He knew there was practically zero chance that the cops had left the beer there but you never knew.

"Fuck it," he muttered and walked home.

He already had one unpleasant conversation that day and another was looming. As he walked past the duplexes on the right, it was not Chapin and his somber song that he heard coming from a window but instead the good ole' boy-voice of Ronnie Van Zant singing about how sick he felt inside.

I've seen a lot of people who thought they were cool But then again, Lord, I've seen a lot of fools

"Me to Ronnie. Me too," Nick said.

A few minutes later, he walked into the house and kicked off his boots. He looked into the living room (might as well get this over with) but his mom was not there.

He headed into the kitchen at the rear of the house but she was not there either. "Nick? That you?" He heard her coming down the stairs as he took a seat at the kitchen table. It was one of the holdover pieces of furniture from the old house and had seen better days. One of the legs was always loose, and you had to be careful not to knock the whole thing over when you sat down.

As he waited, Nick took a good look around the room and, maybe for the first time, noticed just how much work it needed. The kitchen probably hadn't been painted in 10 years, and there was a growing water spot in the far corner of the ceiling. The back door, which led to a small but overgrown yard, was hard to close in the summer when the heat expanded the wood.

And that depressing assessment didn't even include the outdated appliances. "I thought I heard you come in," his mom said. She stood at the opposite end of the table.

"Have a seat mom."

"What's wrong?" She sat in the chair furthest from Nick and started nervously tapping her chin with both thumbs. When you lived the life Ellen Sampson had, you were always anticipating bad news. And you were rarely disappointed.

"They found a body near the tracks today right by the Kingston plant," he said.

She went on tapping her chin and waited.

"It's a long story, but I've spent some time in this spot where the guy turned up. One thing led to another and DeFazio suspended me for a week."

Ellen was trying to connect the dots between the things Nick said. It made no sense.

"What?"

"I told you it's a long story mom. It doesn't matter. But I'm going to be a little light next pay."

"A little? Nick that will be half your pay. You know I need that money." And then it hit her. "This is drinking related right?" Nick said nothing. "I knew it. Jesus Nick."

Nick, who had already endured one of the longest days of his life, was in no mood for a lecture.

"You really want to go there mom? You sure?"

Nick loved his mom, whether she loved him or not (and he honestly was not sure) and rarely lashed out at her. No matter how pissed off he became he normally kept it to himself. But the events of the day were making it increasingly hard to keep his emotions in check. He felt like he was about to blow.

"And what is that supposed to mean Nick? If you have something to say, just say it." It was right there on the tip of his tongue. The pills. The lies. All of it.

You're an addict mom. You're as bad as anyone I've ever seen, and I've seen some shit. You couldn't go a day without those pills. I've seen you shaking like a wet dog when I was 30 minutes late getting back from the pharmacy. You've got some nerve talking about my drinking. You want to see someone with a problem, mom? Take a good look in the mirror.

But Nick said none of those things. He said nothing at all. He got up from the table and left the room.

CHAPTER SIXTEEN

Nick went up to his bedroom and slammed the door. He wanted a beer more than anything but wouldn't give her the satisfaction. He laid on his bed for a while and decided to call Gina and tell her what happened.

Her mom answered the phone and told him Gina was at work and wouldn't be home for a few hours. Did he want her to have Gina call him back? Sure, he said.

With nothing better to do, he reached under his bed and pulled out the manilla folder with "Peter" inside. As was his habit, he read the whole thing through while he debated where to take the story next. *Why am I even doing this*, he thought. *There's no way I'd ever let anyone read it anyway.*

Still, there was something calming about throwing himself into someone else's life (and problems) for a little while, even if that person didn't actually exist.

He took the folder over to the little desk in the corner and sat down. He grabbed a pencil and began tapping it against his chin (he would have been shocked at how much he looked like his mom while he was telling her about his suspension) and then inspiration struck.

He wrote:

You might wonder what Peter's mother thinks about this aspect of his problems. Well so do I. She doesn't seem to think it's a problem because she supplies his money for the beer whenever it's necessary. She's a former alcoholic herself, so I think she's handling it brilliantly. I have no idea where he gets the money that he does have. Anything he had saved from his last job must surely have evaporated by now. All I can say for sure is that on Fridays he comes up with the money without fail.

So I ask myself what to do and what will become of Peter. Trying to predict his future is difficult for me. I want to be optimistic and think something will come along and snap him back into the world of the living. I wish I actually believed that. I think it's going to take some outside help. Peter seems to have lost any desire he may have once had to help himself. Someone is going to have to make a move.

Nick was snapped out of Peter's world by a knock on the door. There was only one person it could be. His mother was not one to be bothered by tension between the two of them, so he knew she wasn't coming to make amends.

"Yeah?"

"My prescription is ready. I was wondering if you'd pick it up." *Should have known*, he thought.

"I'll go over in a little, ok? You're not completely out are you?"

She didn't respond, but Nick could hear her footsteps retreating down the hall and then down the steps.

"That woman is a piece of work," he said to the empty room.

In reality, he wanted to talk to Gina anyway, so the trip to the pharmacy would save him a call later. But first he wanted to keep the momentum he felt he had picked up with the story.

He wrote:

Perhaps his mom should give him an ultimatum: get a job or get out. But it'll never happen. I think he will

*have to be taken by the hand and given a job. If one of
the few people close to him would call and say "Pete, I
found you a job. You'll love it," maybe he would take
it. Then again, maybe he has slipped even further than
I realize. Maybe he would say "No thanks. It would
just interfere with my drinking."*

*I don't know what will become of him. I sit and look at
him and worry. And wonder if he's even Peter
anymore at all.*

o o o

During some of her shifts at the pharmacy, Gina
would stock shelves and take care of other tasks
out on the store's sales floor. When Nick caught
her during one of those times, he could hang
around and talk to her for a little while she
worked. Her manager, Bruce, was pretty easy
going. Even Gina, who liked almost no one,
thought he was ok.

But during other shifts, Gina would spend the
entire eight hours running the cash register and
would not be able to chat.

Because he never knew what he would find her
doing on any given day, Nick waited until about
30 minutes before the end of her shift to head to

the Revco. That way, even if she was "ringing" he could just wait until she was done and walk her home.

Even before he walked into the store, he spotted her at the cashier's station through the large floor-to-ceiling windows. She had three customers in line, so Nick waved and walked over to the pharmacy counter. He paid for his mom's meds (shaking his head at how expensive they had become recently) and motioned to Gina that he would be waiting outside.

It was early November, and most of the days and nights still felt more like fall than winter, but there was a stiff chill in the air. Winter would not be kept at bay for much longer. He sat on the curb in front of the store and watched customers come and go. Most paid him little mind.

Just before Gina's shift ended at 9 o'clock, Scott Lynch got out of his car and was headed into the store when he spotted Nick. He walked over. Lynch had graduated high school with Nick and worked in Avon's tax office. They were far from friends but would shoot the shit from time to time if their paths crossed. Avon was not that big, and both men liked an occasional beer, so it happened fairly often.

"You need a little cup or people won't know where to put the change, Nick," Lynch joked.

"Good one."

Lynch sat down on the curb beside him.

"I heard about the excitement over by the plant today. Crazy huh?"

Nick wasn't surprised that word was already spreading about the body. It wasn't the kind of thing that happened every day in Avon. The tax offices were right down the hall from the police station in the municipal building, so Scott probably knew about it before Nick did.

"Any word on who the guy is?" Nick asked. "Is he local?"

"I haven't heard. Just that he was a hobo."

"Huh?"

"You know, a panhandler. Homeless. You didn't see the body when they took him away?"

"No. I was in the building. The ambulance was gone when I got out there."

Nick left out the part about the nest and the cops' questions about his possible involvement. Nick didn't believe Burrows actually thought he had anything to do with it, but the fact that the dead guy was apparently holding the photo of Nick and his family had his wind up. Burrows only said that he'd be in touch if he had more questions and then sent Nick back into the plant.

"Apparently the guy smelled as bad as he looked," Lynch said. "One less vagrant in the world."

"Your compassion is overwhelming Scott."

Lynch got up and stretched his legs. Nick heard his back pop. "I'll let you know if I hear anything more. Have a good night, Nick." Scott walked into the store.

A few minutes later, the interior store lights went out, and a minute after that Gina, Bruce and two other employees walked out. Bruce pulled a massive key ring off his belt and locked the door.

Gina walked over and plopped down in the same spot Scott Lynch had been sitting in a few minutes earlier.

"What a day," she said.

"Wresting more would-be-thieves?"

"No such luck. Just the usual — people bitching about the prices and our selection. Like it's my fault we only stock Newports and not Newport Lights. Shouldn't be smoking anyway, lady."

Nick chucked. "Yeah, I had a fun day too. That's actually why I stopped."

"Wanna walk?"

"Sure."

Gina started to get up but then stopped. "Oh one thing. The company is having a picnic Saturday out at Idlewild. I've got two free tickets if you want to go." Nick just looked at her.

"I know, it's a kiddie park, but it's free admission and free food. They're raffling off some stuff. Might be fun," she said.

Nick didn't respond.

"Something different anyway. I'm just thrilled to get a weekend day off."

"Free booze?"

Gina sighed. "Root beer is as close as you'll get."

Nick stood up and heard his knees pop as he did. *Maybe Scott wasn't the only one already getting old at 25,* he thought.

"Sure, why not. I have a lot of free time on my hands this week anyway."

"What do you mean?"

"Let's walk."

As they did, he told her about his day — the cops, the nest, the body, the suspension and the fight with his mom. He only left out the part about the photo.

But Gina was far from stupid and eventually asked how the police tied Nick to the nest.

He just shrugged it off. "No idea."

Nick wasn't really sure why he was holding back the part about the photo, but he just couldn't bring himself to talk about it. It felt like some kind of personal violation that the guy had found that picture.

"So now you're drinking right in the plant huh? I guess it was only a matter of time."

"It was one beer one time. I don't know how the old man even found the can. Just dumb luck."

"Right," she said.

They walked in silence for a few minutes and eventually stopped in front of the Marino house. Nick was ready to get home. It had been a long day and he was exhausted. He figured his mom would be getting antsy about her meds too.

"So Saturday?" she asked.

"Yeah, sure."

"Who's driving?"

He just shook his head. "I'll be here at 9."

o o o

Idlewild Highlands sat about an hour east of Avon on state Route 22. It was a popular family destination in the summer, and the park had added a "fall festival" to its autumn calendar within the past few years to keep those Pittsburgh dollars flowing into the local economy for a couple of additional weeks. The Sampsons normally spent a day at

Kennywood, Pittsburgh's larger amusement park, in the spring, and, at least when Nick was small, a day at Idlewild in the summer.

The park was split into two distinct parts: The more traditional side, featuring "thrill" rides targeted primarily at small children, games of chance (ring toss, baseball toss, beanbag toss) and concession stands. On the other side of the property sat Storybook Woodlands. There, guests could take a winding, walking tour through life size recreations of a dozen or so fairy tales.

Nick could remember starring in wonder at the massive, two-story wooden depiction of an open story book through which visitors passed to gain access to the park. From there, one of the first stops along the trail through the woods was the wall on which Humpty Dumpty sat. It was built low enough to the ground that parents could prop their kids beside Humpty and snap a quick photo. In fact, unbeknownst to Nick, there was a picture in the shoe box beneath his mom's bed showing him at age four gazing warily at the legendary, cracked egg.

Nick and Gina first checked in at the pavilion her company was using as its base for the day. Volunteers were busy spreading cold cuts, macaroni salad, fried chicken and watermelon on a long, cloth-covered table. A second table was already loaded with cakes, pies, cookies and other desserts.

"Where to first?" he asked. Nick had little interest in the rides but was curious to get a look at the attractions on the Storybook side. It had been ages since he'd been there, but he suspected little had changed.

"The Red Rocket," Gina said.

"Please, no," Nick said.

Gina whacked him on the shoulder.

"Baby. Let's go."

The Rocket was far and away the most daunting of the rides in the park. Nick didn't mind roller coasters, and the Rocket's hills were not especially high (not compared to Kennywood's Thunderbolt, anyway). His concern was that the thing always looked like it was on the verge of collapse. *A sparrow landing on the wrong section of rail could bring this whole thing down,* he thought as they approached the entrance.

Nick stopped Gina as she started up the ride's entrance ramp. "How do the Catholics do that thing?" Nick asked as he mimed making the sign of the cross on his forehead and shoulders.

"You did it backward, but I think you'll be ok. This thing has been running for 100 years."

"That's exactly my concern," he said.

Five minutes later, they were both laughing as they exited the ride. Nick had to admit (to himself) he was having a good time, and he thought the diversion might have been exactly what he needed given the events of earlier in the week.

"Ah, back on terra firma," he said as they pushed through the swinging gate at the bottom of the exit. "I wasn't sure I'd ever be able to say that again."

"I wish you wouldn't have said it the first time," she said. "Who talks like that?"

After a quick bathroom break, Nick told Gina he wanted to get a look at the Storybook side of the park. They were already walking in that direction. He had some fuzzy memories of having been there with his dad. He was sure his mom was with them too, but it was his dad he could picture in his mind's eye.

In particular, he remembered one little house along the twisted path through the woods that a younger version of Nick did not want to enter. Inside, the Big Bad Wolf laid in bed in all his (plastic) glory wearing Grandmas clothes. The sharp white teeth revealed by its perpetual, wicked smile were enormous. *"It's just make-believe," Ed Sampson told his youngest boy. "It's not real." Nick resisted. Ed reached down and took his hand. "It's fine Nicky. I won't let anything hurt you."* "Sure, Nick, we can head over there" she said. They were strolling down a winding, blacktop path with century-old oaks lining both sides. The trees were changing colors, and Nick kicked a few yellow and orange leaves that were scattered across the path as they walked. There were gaming stands on the left.

"But one more stop first," Gina said, and walked over to a booth that held a ring-toss game. For a dollar, players got three chances to throw a red, pie-sized ring around one of the hundreds of glass bottles that sat on the gaming floor. They looked like Kingston bottles. Nick knew from experience the game was much harder than it looked. But hanging along the rear wall of the booth were large, plush animals that went to the winners.

"Win me one of those," Gina said. She was pointing to a big blue unicorn with an orange horn hanging on a hook in the corner. "That would look great in my room."

Nick stopped. "Win you one?" "What? You can't do it?

"Of course I can. But that's the kind of thing a girl would say to her boyfriend," he said.

Nick tried to remember the exact wording Gina had used that night at the Dairy Delite.

"This isn't a date, Gina."

o   o   o

Hours later, they walked out to the car. Gina didn't win anything at the booths, but she did win something called a videocassette recorder at the company's raffle. The thing apparently played movies on your home TV or something.

All in all it had been a good day.

As they neared the car, Gina stopped.

Nick didn't even notice until after he climbed in the driver's side. He saw her standing 50 feet down the gravel lot. She had set the box holding the recorder on the ground. He got back out and approached her.

"What are you doing?" he asked.

"Tell me you weren't drinking. No bullshit, Nick. Yes or no?"

"What? There wasn't even any beer here. You know that. I don't know..."

He stopped. Was he really going to feed her this crap? He was so tired of all the acting. Of all the fucking lies. Besides, she clearly knew anyway.

He reached inside his jacket and pulled out a half pint bottle of vodka. It was empty. He dropped it

at his feet, reached into his other pocket and
pulled out his keys.

He tossed them to her.

CHAPTER SEVENTEEN

"How did you know?"

"You were walking like a sailor on shore leave," Gina said. "I'm disappointed in myself for not seeing it earlier." Nick said nothing.

"Explain this to me. Help me to understand, Nick. I'm serious. Why did you bring the vodka?"

They were headed west toward Avon on route 22. Traffic was light on the two-lane road.

"My grandfather was a drunk," he said.

Gina waited for him to go on but he just sat there.

"Your mom's dad?"

"No. Well, actually, maybe him too. I don't know much about him, other than that he worked at Kopp Glass. I meant my dad's dad, but honestly I don't know much about him

either." "Ok."

"The day my dad left us he took me over to the milk store for ice cream sandwiches first. Some stuff he wanted to tell me I guess. Anyway, we saw a bum staggering around and he said the guy reminded him of his old man."

Gina wasn't sure what to say, but she wanted to keep Nick talking. He hardly ever opened up, especially about his family.

"So the heavy drinking is like a family tradition or something?"

He chuckled. "Some tradition huh? Actually, I'm wondering if it skips a generation or something. Because my dad never drank at all. At least not that I can remember."

Gina kept the speedometer right at 45. There were few other cars on the road, but at that time of year a deer was apt to dart out in front of you. And she was in no hurry to get back.

She thought about what Nick had told her.

"I think you got it wrong, Nick," she said.

He reached over and turned the volume on the radio down a little.

"How do you mean?"

"I don't think the drinking skips a generation. I think your dad didn't drink because he was so disgusted by what he saw of his own dad. Maybe he didn't want to end up like

that."

Nick nodded. "I never really thought about that. Could be. He wasn't around by the time I would have started noticing stuff like that, though. At 12, I'm not sure I was keeping a close eye on my parents eating and drinking habits."

In his mind's eye, Nick saw his dad standing in the backyard of their old house. He was wearing white shorts and a deep blue T-shirt that was a size too small. He was holding a golf club. Ten-year-old Nick stood at the top of the two short steps that led down to the sunken back porch. He was wearing a baseball glove on his right hand. "Whenever you're ready!" he yelled to his dad. The two had concocted the game (it had no name) a month or so earlier. His dad loved golf and Nick was a budding hockey fan, and the "sport" was a hybrid that allowed them both a little practice.

And a little time together.

Ed lined up a small plastic golf ball and used a 5-iron to drive it toward the house. His goal was to smack the ball between two of the posts that held up the roof over the back porch. Nick's job was to stop it.

The shot was ticketed for the corner above Nick's right shoulder, but at the last second the baseball glove appeared. He caught it.

"Nice save Nick," Ed yelled.

He reached for another ball and prepared the next shot.

There was a can sitting just beyond the little collection of plastic balls. A little refreshment for a hot summer day. But what was in it? Nick wasn't sure, but he thought it was Pepsi.

"You would have known," Gina said. A tractor-trailer carrying a load of huge logs passed them going in the other direction. "But the question you have to ask yourself is where does this all leave you?"

Yep, that's the question all right, Nick thought. He looked out the passenger window and could see nothing but trees. It was mesmerizing watching the forest fly by. Autumn in Western Pennsylvania was in its full glory. He hadn't noticed a home or even a barn for 10 minutes, and they wouldn't hit the next town for 10 more. While part of his mind was wondering how he could have been stupid enough to take the bottle into the park, another part was taking inventory of the booze he had waiting for him at home. *This sucks,* he thought.

He was about to ask Gina if she wanted to stop for a bite to eat somewhere along the way, when he heard (and felt) the car hit the rumble strips on the left side of the road. He looked over at Gina and his heart trim hammered:

She was having a seizure.

Jesus! his mind screamed. *Not now!*

Nick reached over and yanked the wheel to bring the car back into the center of the west bound side of the road. They had drifted out of their lane and completely across the east bound side of the highway. If it wasn't for the rumble strips, Nick was sure they would have slammed into the guard rail and probably flipped over it and fell down into the gulley below.

Gina stared straight ahead, mumbling quietly. There was a thin line of drool dripping from the corner of her mouth. She never blinked. Her hands gripped the wheel tightly, and Nick struggled to keep the car centered. He was able to do it, but that was only half the problem. Gina's foot was still on the gas pedal.

She did not seem to be increasing pressure on the pedal (*that's one break*, Nick's frantic mind thought) but neither did she seem to be easing on it. Nick was quickly trying to decide what to do, but the 8 ounces of vodka in his system was not helping. He thought he could either try to ride it out — control the steering wheel and hope she didn't suddenly accelerate — until Gina came out of the seizure, or he could try to gain control of the foot pedals himself.

He quickly decided on the latter. He scooted across the bench seat until he was pressed tightly up against Gina, hip to hip. He moved his left foot into the driver's footwell and knocked Gina's foot off the gas. Nick tried to then use his right foot to pin Gina's feet against the center console. But as he did, Gina suddenly yanked the wheel hard to the left.

"Fuck Gina no!" he yelled.

As he fought for control of the wheel, he managed to get his left foot on the brake. Nick glanced down into the footwell for a split second to see where Gina's feet were as the car began to slow. But he miscalculated the bend in the road, and the car's left side scraped along the guard rail, throwing up sparks. "Fuck!" Nick screamed. He pulled the wheel to the left to once again center the car in the right lane. He had the speed down to a crawl. About 100 yards ahead, he saw lights signaling an establishment of some sort on the right. He pulled into the parking lot (it was a restaurant, he noticed), put the car in park and killed the engine.

Nick moved back over to his side of the car, and his breathing and heart rate began to return to something approaching normal. "Jesus, that was close," he said.

Gina was starting to come around. There was always a brief period of "awakening" after a seizure as she slowly realized when and where she was.

"Why are we stopped?"

He just looked at her and shook his head.

"Slide over," he said. "I'm driving."

o   o   o

Thirty minutes later Nick pulled up in front of the Marino home. There was a light on beyond the large front window, which Nick knew looked into the spacious living room.

Talk had been at a minimum during the second half of the drive home. Nick wasn't sure what to say. He felt guilty for his role in the accident, but part of him was pissed at Gina too. He knew she had a license and did what she could to keep the seizures under control. But still.

"Look, I'm sorry about the drinking. I had a good time out there today." Gina shook her head and sighed.

"We're quite a pair, aren't we? An epileptic and an alcoholic."

He looked over at Gina, and they both started laughing as her words hit home.

"Yes indeed," he said.

Nick registered that it was the first time he had ever heard her use the word "epileptic."

Actually, it was the first time she had used the word "alcoholic" too, at least as it pertained to Nick. He wasn't sure what to think of that.

"So we're good?" he asked.

She gave him a little half smile as she opened the door.

"Yeah, Nick, we're good."

He jumped out and opened the trunk. He grabbed the videocasette recorder and carried it up onto the porch.

"Want me to take it in?"

"No I got it. Thanks," she said. "I'll talk to you tomorrow." She pulled out her key and let herself in.

Nick stood on the porch for a minute, then got into the car and headed home.

o   o   o

Two days later, on Monday morning, Nick was in his room serving his work suspension when he heard a knock on the front door. He paid no attention until his mom began calling from the downstairs hall a minute later.

"Yeah?"

"Can you come down?"

Nick threw the hockey magazine he'd been reading on the bed and walked down the steps.

Seated across the living room from his mom was officer Burrows.

He was wearing his police uniform, and Nick noticed that his shoes looked like they had been recently shined. It clearly wasn't a social call.

"Hi, Nick," he said. "Can we talk a minute?"

Miranda rights, he's going to read me my Miranda rights, Nick thought. *I have a right to an attorney and to remain silent.* A million old cop shows started playing in his head.

Nick was clueless as to why he felt so guilty. Clearly, he had done nothing wrong. Well, other than drinking on the job, that was.

And that reminded him of something.

"How did you know I was home?" he asked the cop.

Burrows had a little yellow notepad on his lap. He flipped a page.

"I didn't. I went to the plant and they told me I'd probably find you here." Nick snorted.

"Are you going to arrest me for drinking in public? I hope you have some proof." "Nick," his mom said. She shot him a look.

"It's ok ma'am," Burrows said. He looked back at Nick. "No, Nick, I'm not here for that, although I wouldn't advise continuing it, if you have been." He seemed to think of something else. "I noticed the damage on your car out there. Hope you weren't drinking and driving."

Oh thanks a lot pal, Nick thought. He had not yet got around to telling his mom about the drive home from Idlewild. He looked over, and she shot him another look, the latter one could have melted ice.

"It's nothing mom," he said. Nick was absently fingering the seagull hanging on the cheap chain around his neck. It was a nervous tic he had picked up recently, although he was completely unaware of it.

She ignored Nick and looked at Burrows. "I'm sorry officer. I should have asked if you'd like coffee or something," Ellen said. "Forgive me. It'll just take a minute." She started to get up, but Burrows motioned her back to the couch.

Nick thought she looked like she already had too much coffee in her system. Or maybe she was behind schedule for her next dose of pills. She was having as much trouble sitting still as Nick was.

"No, thank you," Burrows said. "I only have a minute." He looked down at his pad again, and the grandfather clock in the corner chimed to mark the half hour.

"I wanted to tell you about the situation we investigated the other day on Waverly," he hesitated. "The body, I mean." Again, he flipped a page. Nick thought it as all for show, but for whose benefit?

"Anyway, it appears that the subject was struck by a train as he attempted to cross the tracks. We don't know where he was coming from or where he was headed. There are

still a lot of questions."

Nick was waiting for his mom to shout, "*see, I told you to watch those trains!*" but she sat still as stone and said nothing.

He noticed that he and his mom were not the only nervous people in the room. Burrows looked uneasy too. There were fine sweat beads forming just below his hairline.

The cop hesitated a beat and then looked from Nick to his mom.

"Actually, I'm glad you're both here," he said. "My captain told me to look for Nick at work, but you both need to hear this. We have a positive ID on the body." With that, time stood still for Nick. Each second marked by the grandfather clock's small, gold hand seemed to last an hour.

Because he suddenly knew.

Beyond a shadow of a doubt, *he knew* what Burrows was about to say.

Nick decided to beat him to it.

"It's my dad," Nick said. It was not a question.

Burrows looked from Nick to Ellen and then back again.

"No, Nick," he said. It's Nevin."

CHAPTER EIGHTEEN

Word of Nevin Sampson's return to Avon and subsequent, unfortunate demise spread across town like wildfire.

From the counter at the Village Dairy to the stools at the Circus Bar to the checkout lines at the A&P, Avonites (an unfortunate moniker if there ever was one, Nick thought) seemingly could talk of little else.

That grapevine that Gina had mentioned to Nick a few months before? It was running on all cylinders. And who could blame the townsfolk?

It wasn't every day that a mysterious body turned up in town that happened to have been struck by a train and, oh yeah, turned out to be the long-lost younger brother of one of the town's war heroes.

Nate's name was right there on the war memorial in front of the library on Monongahela Street (not far from the Dairy Delite) with hundreds of other Avon boys who had served their country in various wars.

Speculation about Nevin — where he had been all those years and what brought him back to Avon

— ran from the ridiculous to the absurd. One hypothesis that was gaining steam proposed that Nevin had actually been living in town the whole time under an alias. Facial injuries suffered during his time in Vietnam and plastic surgery kept anyone from recognizing him.

Others said he had joined the circus.

But a conversation between two old-timers sitting on a bench outside the elementary school might have come closest to the truth.

Ed Martini, who at one time drove a school bus in town, said that he had spoken with quite a few boys who had returned from the war in Vietnam. Many of them relayed to Martini that they feared some of the atrocities they had seen (and, in some cases, took part in) would stay with them for a long, long time.

They didn't teach anything at boot camp that could prepare 19-year-old boys for the sickening realities that smacked them in the face every day, they said.

And, to add insult to injury, their own country not only seemed indifferent to their struggles, but in some cases treated their return home as a personal afront. It made reincorporating back into civilized society a monumental challenge.

For some, it was impossible.

"But Nevin was a photographer," said Clarence Voigt, Martini's bench mate that day. "He wasn't a soldier."

Martini watched a school bus turn down Hayes Street. It looked very similar to the one he drove decades earlier.

"My guess is that he was right there in the middle of it," Martini said. "He wasn't shooting a rifle, but the spatter was still landing on him."

o o o

After showing Burrows to the door, Nick went back into the living room to sit with his mom. Burrows' revelation had rocked them both. Nick's mind was going a thousand miles an hour and in 10 different directions, and he didn't know what to say.

He could only imagine what his mom was going through. First, she lost Nate. Then Ed left her high and dry. She then spent years mourning Nevin, only to find out he had been close enough to touch. And now this.

"Jesus," was all he got out.

He looked at his mom, but she seemed oddly calm. *Maybe this is finally giving her some closure,* Nick thought. Because as tragic as Nate's death was, at least there had been a body to bury. Until that day, that had not been the case with Nevin.

"You want to talk mom?" he asked.

The TV was playing (Nick thought it was the soap opera Love of Life) and Ellen was looking at it, but he imagined she was actually seeing something from years ago. Images of a younger Nevin, no doubt, were running through her mind.

"Yes, but not right now, Nicky," she said. "I'm actually thinking of going for a walk. I need some fresh air to clear my head."

Nick thought that was a great idea. He wished she would get out much more often than she did. Her trips outside mainly consisted of walking up the street to Granna's Market (maybe once a week) and going out to the mailbox (daily). Other than that, not much.

"Ok, great," he said. "I'll be upstairs. I didn't sleep real well last night so I might take a nap. But come up when you're back."

"I will."

Nick plodded up the stairs and fell back into his bed. He had not been lying about his lack of sleep the night before.

Because the panic had come back.

It appeared out of virtually nowhere and escalated at a frightening pace. He had been absently gazing through a magazine when an image inside reminded him of a covered bridge outside of Pocataw. From there, his mind took him back to his most recent visit to the vacation town and then quickly flipped through a series of images ending with one of Nick standing at the balcony railing outside his room at the Poolside Motel.

His heart began to race.

Satan. Lucifer. Beelzebub.

What did Regan do in The Exorcist that led to her possession, he wondered wildly? Maybe she had a panic-fueled obsession with the devil. Maybe she, like Nick, just couldn't stop thinking about it, and so Satan used that as an opening? How would he know if he was being possessed? What would it initially feel like?

Maybe it would feel just...like...this, his mind whispered.

He jumped off the bed and ran for the door. He had to get out.

It took every ounce of mental strength he could muster, and he rode the panic coaster for more than two hours, but Nick did not leave the room.

o   o   o

Nick was drifting off not long after he left his mom downstairs, when the phone rang. There was one in the kitchen and another on a small table in the upstairs hallway. A minute later his mom rapped softly on his door.

"I wouldn't bother you except that it was Mr. DeFazio on the phone, Nick. He asked if you could head down there."

"Ok, thanks mom."

He had no idea what the old man wanted but based on the events of recent days he figured it couldn't be good. The next piece of positive news he got would be the first in a long, long time.

He took his time getting dressed, then slowly walked down Waverly toward Kingston.

When he entered the building, he spotted Freddy Baxter counting pallets of full cases nearby. He saw Nick and motioned him up the steps to where the "executive offices" were. Noise from the plant's equipment would have made it impossible to hear Freddy even from that short distance.

He knocked on the door to the office but figured they'd never hear it and let himself in. There was a small desk where, Charlene, Dean's secretary usually sat, but she wasn't there. Mr. DeFazio was in the office alone and motioned Nick into the chair where he had sat less than a week before.

I probably hadn't been in here in a year and now it's twice within a week, Nick thought as he sat.

"I'll make this quick," DeFazio said as soon as Nick was seated. "I heard about Nevin. I'm sorry Nick."

How in the hell did he hear that already? Nick wondered. *I just found out myself a few hours ago. The old man must have ears all over town.*

"Anyway, I don't want to add any stress for you and your mom so I'm reinstating you immediately. Head down to the floor and ask Freddy where he needs you."

Nick was about to point out that he wasn't dressed for work but thought better of it. His regular clothes were maybe a step above the rags he wore to work. Maybe half a step. He said "thanks" instead. Nick got up and reached the office door when DeFazio stopped him.

"One other thing. I already contacted Neid's. I'm going pay for the funeral and burial."

Jesus everything was happening so fast. Nick hadn't even thought about having to make arrangements for Nevin.

"Oh, ok. Wow. Thanks. That's very nice of you," Nick said. "I haven't talked to my mom about any of that but I'm sure she's not going to want to have a full-blown funeral." The more he thought about it the surer he was. "Yeah, no way she's gonna want to do that."

"Whatever you want. And if you need to take some time off of work that's fine." He seemed to realize the irony of his words, given Nick's recent suspension. "I mean with full pay of course.

Nick headed back down to the work floor. Baxter saw him coming and he clearly already knew about the change in Nick's work status.

"Go replace Davis on the slitter. Tell him to come see me."

Nick didn't reply but just gave him a thumbs up and headed deeper into the building. As he maneuvered under and around the production line, he noticed they were bottling black grape.

At the slitter, he found Tom Davis frantically cleaning up the results of a crash. He saw Nick coming.

"You back?"

"Yep. Go see Baxter." He bent over to help Tom get the mess cleaned up. The line was stopped and heads would roll if it stayed that way for long. "How's she running?"

Davis just smiled. "Have fun," he said.

o o o

He finished the shift (the slitter operated surprisingly well. Nick thought maybe it missed him) and headed home. He gave the nest a glance as he passed but continued up the potholed road.

He noticed the mail was still in the mailbox attached to the front of the house, which was unusual, so he grabbed it and went inside.

His mom was lying face down in the hallway between the living room and kitchen. "Mom!" Nick screamed. He ran over, turned her onto her back and checked to see if she was breathing. For a moment, some old advice about not moving an injured person ran through his head, but it was too late to worry about that. He wasn't positive, but he thought he could see her chest rising and falling.

Just beyond her outstretched left hand was a pill bottle. Nick grabbed it and was not surprised to find that it was empty.

"God mom what the fuck!"

The kitchen phone was hanging on the wall directly over his head. He grabbed the handset — almost yanked the whole thing off the wall in the process — and dialed 911.

o o o

The ambulance arrived in about eight minutes (Nick knew because he counted each one of them along with the grandfather clock in the corner) and the EMTs had his mom secured in the back of the vehicle 10 minutes after that. Nick kept asking them if she was going to be ok, but both men were focused on the task of taking her vitals and getting her safely onto the gurney. Still, the fact that they kept deflecting his questions did nothing to ease Nick's mind.

"You mentioned pills," one of the techs said to Nick as they were preparing to head outside.

"Yeah, here." He had shoved the empty bottle into his pocket. He pulled it out and handed it over. "Which hospital?"

"Braddock," tech #1 said.

"Really?" The hospital's less-than-stellar reputation was well known by everyone in Avon. The joke in the area was that you could get end-of-life care not only at the hospice next door but at the hospital itself too.

"It's closest," the tech said. "We need to get moving." The men started maneuvering the gurney through the narrow hallway. It was a tight fit. "You coming with us? There's room in the back."

"No, but I'll be right behind you," Nick said.

o o o

Nick stood on the porch in the failing afternoon light and watched the ambulance pull away. Its lights were flashing but the siren was quiet, at least so far. He thought about what a crazy day it had been. Burrows, DeFazio and the coup de grace — his mom's apparent attempt at suicide.

It was probably a bad idea to show up at a hospital smelling like booze, but in that moment Nick did not give a fuck. He went into the kitchen and pulled out a beer.

He chugged.

o o o

Three more beers and Nick felt mellow enough to face the rest of the day, whatever it held. He thought it was already the longest day of his life. He grabbed his keys off the mantle and was heading out when the phone in the kitchen started ringing.

He looked at it for a second and was just going to let it ring when it occurred to him that it might be the hospital with news about his mom.

"Fuck me," he said.

He walked down the hallway and plucked the handset off the wall.

"Hello?"

"Nick?"

"Yeah. Who's this?" "Scott."

"Um, which Scott?" Nick actually could not think of anyone he knew by that name.

"Lynch."

Nick made the connection. He had seen Scott in the Revco parking lot the other night while he waited for Gina.

"Oh, sorry Scott. Long day. I actually can't talk. Long story."

"I know," Lynch said. "And I know something else."

Nick waited a beat, but there was silence from the other end of the line.

"I'm listening. And can you speak up? Why are you whispering?"

"I'm at work. Listen, Nick. You did not hear this from me, but the cops have something you'll want to see. Go see Burrows, but keep my name out of it."

The line went dead

CHAPTER NINETEEN

Nick hung up. He thought about immediately walking over to the police station but had to make sure his mom was ok first. As he drove to the hospital, his mind kept returning to one thing Scott had said. *"cops have something.."* What could it possibly be? Then he remembered the photo. Scott probably found out about the family picture that the homeless guy had been holding. Lynch didn't realize the photo was already in the nest.

The trip to the hospital took less than 10 minutes. The town of Braddock, where the hospital sat, was named after some long-ago war general, Nick thought. The guy had fought in the French and Indian War, or maybe it was the Revolutionary War? Nick wasn't sure. But either way, what was the connection to the local area? Were either of those wars fought in Western Pennsylvania? *Should have paid better attention in history class*, Nick thought.

To say that Braddock had seen better days would be a massive understatement. The town was the personification of urban blight. Crumbling, closed up storefronts accounted for about 75% of Main

Street, and Nick noticed only a handful of establishments that were open. Those included a bakery, a tire store and a pawn shop. And, of course, the bars.

Nick hardly spent any time there, but the first thing he thought about whenever he was in Braddock was his dad telling him about the incredible high school football team it fielded in the 1950s. The team had rolled off just short of 50 consecutive wins, his dad said.

He didn't know if the French and Indian War was fought there, but he knew the record of Braddock's football team from 20 years earlier. *Crazy how the mind works*, Nick thought.

He parked, entered the hospital and headed for the emergency ward. A nurse at the desk told him that his mom was still being examined.

"How is she?" he asked.

"Are you next of kin?"

"I'm her son."

"Well you can head on back if you want. I don't have any information about her condition yet."

Nick hesitated. He really didn't want to see her like that — tubes snaking all over her body and probably an oxygen mask on her pale face. Would it make him a horrible son if he waited a little? *What are you really afraid of Nick?* the little voice in his head asked. *You think she's dead, don't you? And then that will leave...well, that will leave just you, right Nick?*

"Would it be ok if I waited out here?"

"Sure, I'll let you know as soon as I have any information. There's coffee over there in the corner," the nurse said.

Nick took a seat in the waiting area. A few minutes later he fell asleep.

o o o

"Sir?"

"Huh?" Nick woke to a nurse in light blue uniform gently tapping his shoulder. It took him a minute to get his bearings, but then he remembered. The hospital. "Oh. Sorry. I guess I drifted off."

"You are Mrs. Sampson's son, right?"

"Yes." Nick was slowly coming out of the fog. He was going to grab a cup of coffee (and head to the bathroom, those four beers were simmering) as soon as the nurse left.

"They just took your mom upstairs. They're going to keep her overnight, but she's going to be ok," she said.

Relief flooded Nick's system. More than he would have believed possible before the whole ordeal began.

"Oh thank God," he said. "Is there anything else you can you tell me?"

"The doctor will be in to see her shortly. He can answer your questions then." She looked down at a clipboard she was holding. "She's in room 3208."

o o o

He went to the bathroom and then grabbed a cup of coffee before getting on the elevator. He thought about just taking the stairs (Nick was not crazy about elevators, or escalators for that matter) but he was worried about spilling the coffee. Bright green signs with red arrows pointed visitors to the patient rooms, and Nick found 3208 with no trouble.

But he hesitated before going in.

Be a man Nick for once in your fucking life. Get in there, that voice in his head said.

Nick thought it sounded like his dad. *For God's sake, Nate fought in Vietnam and you can't even face your* (dying, she's dying) *mother?*

He would have probably stayed locked in place a little longer regardless, but he heard a voice coming from inside the room. He opened the door and saw a man in a white coat leaning over the room's lone bed. His mom looked just as he feared she would: face drained of all color, hair askew and her frail body hooked up to all sorts of hospital equipment that filled the room with beeps and hums.

He entered the room and closed the door but stood just inside it. A minute later, the guy walked over and motioned Nick to the hallway outside.

"Are you her son?" It was already the third time since he arrived at the hospital that Nick's identity had been questioned. *I guess it's good that they won't just tell this stuff to random strangers,* he thought and stifled a chuckle. He was clearly losing it.

"Yes, I'm Nick."

"Doctor Anderson," the guy said, and stuck out his hand.

Two attendants slowly pushed a gurney carrying an elderly man along the hall. They stopped two rooms further down.

"Your mom is going to be ok, physically at least," he said. "She took about a half dozen Percocet, but she vomited in the ambulance, which is a good thing. She'll be nauseous and drowsy when she comes around, but she'll be fine in a day or two."

"That's great to hear," Nick said. Then he thought of something else. "You said physically?"

"She's going to need some counseling," the doctor said. He must have seen the perplexed look on Nick's face. "We found another handful of pills in her pocket. If she wanted to..." he paused.

"...finish things I guess, she would have taken them all. We see this all the time."

"So you don't think she was trying to kill herself?" Nick asked.

"My guess? No. People who want to do it usually have little trouble in getting the job done. This was a cry for help," Anderson said.

o o o

Nick had no idea what hours Burrows worked, but the cop had visited Nick and his mom in the morning.

Early the day after his trip to see his mom at the hospital, Nick walked over to the municipal building. The old structure housed the police and fire departments, tax offices, mayor's office and even a notary. Two firetrucks were lined up at the curb.

There was a glass window built into the wall next to the door that the cops used to enter and exit the police offices. Nick walked up and introduced himself to the officer on the other side of the glass.

"I'm Nick Sampson. I'm looking for officer Burrows. He paid me a visit at home yesterday." Nick didn't know if the whole police force knew the details of the cases other cops were working, but he didn't want to say anything more than necessary.

The cop looked bored, and mildly annoyed, but got up and headed into the back. "Hang on," he said.

Nick was expecting a long wait. Heck, they'd probably just wait him out and see if he went away. But two minutes later, Burrows himself opened the door and motioned Nick into the back.

The place looked just as Nick would have imagined, which was to say it looked much like such offices were depicted on TV shows.

When they were seated on opposite sides of Burrow's desk, the cop surprised him again.

"You heard, right?"

Nick was definitely taken off guard. He wasn't sure how he was going to ask about the tip Lynch had given him without mentioning Scott's call, but he thought he would have to broach the subject himself. He did not expect Burrows to do it.

"Um..."

"Don't worry about it," the cop said. "This place is full of leaks, and I don't just mean the ceiling." Nick instinctively looked up and Burrows laughed. "I would have called you later today anyway. I wasn't holding out on you, Nick, we just weren't sure what we had." Nick just sat there.

Burrows reached into one of the desk drawers and pulled out a folded sheaf of yellow papers. He flattened the pages out and set them in front of Nick.

"I'll give you some privacy to read this, but let me first tell you where we are."

"We have positively identified the body as your brother, Nevin. I'll spare you the specifics of how we know. We do not know exactly how long he's been in the area, but some of that is addressed in the letter." He tapped the pages. "But he's been back in the states for three years."

Nick tried hard to keep his mouth from dropping open. Nevin had been missing since 1975, and everyone — the family, his employer, the U.S. government — thought he had died even though his body was never recovered. Burrows was telling him that Nevin had been in the U.S. basically the whole time.

Burrows continued. "Our thinking is that he got clipped while crossing the tracks and hung on until he got into your little apartment there." He saw the look on Nick's face and backtracked. "Ok, whatever. We know you've spent some time in there. Anyway, his injuries would have killed him pretty quickly after he was hit, so I don't think he suffered long."

He looked at Nick to see if he had any questions and then went on.

"I can't imagine what this is like for you and your mom, Nick. So if you need anything let me know." He paused. "I mean that. I'm not a psychologist so I don't know if this letter will help you or not, but it's yours." He pushed it closer to Nick. "We're done with it."

Nick had a thousand questions, but the first one to come to his lips was "How do you know this was for me?" He pointed to the letter.

Burrows chuckled. "I haven't made detective yet, that's true. But I know a good clue when I see it." He turned the top page around so that it was facing Nick. "What's the first word there?" Then he saw it.

It said "Nick."

o o o

"I'll be around if you need me, but take all the time you want," Burrows said. He got up and walked across the squad room. Nick wanted to take the letter home immediately, but his curiosity was overwhelming. He would not be able to wait.

The letter, which ran for nine pages, had clearly been written over a long period of time. Nick wasn't a detective either, but it was obvious different pens and pencils had been used. And the handwriting wasn't consistent throughout. In some places it was clear and legible (and pretty-well written, Nick thought) and in other places some words were hard to make out. Part of it had gotten wet, and the ink was smudged there.

Nick read the whole thing four times (and would read it many more in the coming years) before he called Burrows back over. The letter covered a lot of ground, but there were three main points that Nick took away from it.

First, Nevin still wasn't sure if he would ever approach Nick (or Ellen). That was the reason for the letter. If he decided on a face-to-face at some point, Nevin wrote, he'd throw away the letter. Otherwise, he was going to leave it in the nest and disappear for good.

He had wanted to take a little time to "get his bearings" when he first got back to the states before he approached the family. But the longer he stayed away the harder it became to face them and his old life.

But he had been back in Avon for about six months. And, yes, he had been keeping an eye on Nick from a distance for a little while, and so he knew about the nest. But he never mentioned how he found the photo.

HPrior to returning to Avon, he had wandered around the U.S. after jumping on a military transport late one night in Saigon that landed him in San Francisco.

"It was chaos," Nevin wrote. "It was a miracle I got out. I know a lot of guys who didn't and I have to live with that."

t sounded like a lot of Nevin's time before he turned up in Avon had been spent in Nebraska, for reasons that were not clear. He hinted at one point that there might have been a woman in the picture, and his involvement with her may have led him down some dark alleyways, both literally and figuratively.

Second, Nevin tried to describe some of the things he saw in Vietnam. It was horrific and graphic in places, and was maybe best summed up in a story he related about a helicopter crash.

A Huey had landed in the midst of a firefight to evacuate injured soldiers from the Mekong River Delta. It had taken on about a dozen American casualties and had just lifted off when it was hit by fire from the North Vietnamese on the ground. Apparently, the prop was hit, and the copter spun wildly, crashed to the ground and burst into flames. Nevin, who watched from nearby cover with about 20 other soldiers, said the cargo door flew open and some of the soldiers ran out. They were all on fire. *"As horrible as it was to watch, the sounds and smells were worse. I hear those screams at night sometimes when I'm trying to go to sleep. And on other nights I can even smell burning flesh."*

Third, and most important to Nick, Nevin wrote about a conversation he had with their father before Nevin left for Vietnam. Nevin had been writing about what a coward (and worthless piece of shit) Ed was for running out on Nick when he mentioned the meeting.

That part, Nick read over and over. He was gobsmacked.

Nevin wrote:

He actually showed up on my doorstep late one night right before I shipped out. I have no idea how he found me or how he knew I was leaving. I barely even recognized him. He looked so old. Hell, I hadn't laid eyes on the fucker for 8 years. The third time reading it Nick wondered if maybe Ellen had filled Ed in. Did that mean Ed had never left the state? Was it possible his parents stayed in touch? What other explanation could there be? *He wanted to apologize and to tell me to be safe. Mom had already lost one son over there and all that bullshit. I told him to fuck off and that you were the one he needed to apologize to. For whatever reason that seemed to hit him hard. He turned to walk away but then he goes "Nicky was always my favorite. I loved all you boys but Nicky was..." I couldn't make out the rest because he was down the steps and out of my life again. And good riddance. But I wanted you to know that.*

o o o

Nick was still sitting at the desk an hour later when Burrows came back. When his mom got home from the hospital, the two of them were going to sit down and have a nice chat about what she knew — if anything — about Ed Sampson's current whereabouts. His dad would be about 70, but still. Was it possible that he was alive and well and maybe living not too far from Avon. Or even *in* Avon?

Nick had never felt so confused and bewildered in his life. It must have shown on his face.

"It's a lot, I know," Burrow said. "And we're not done." *Oh God what else?* Nick thought.

"Nevin had a backpack on him with all sorts of stuff — clothes, food, photos from his time in 'Nam, books. Pretty ordinary stuff mostly, and obviously you can have it all. There was one strange item. But first, this."

Burrows reached back into the same drawer he pulled Nevin's letter from earlier and came out with the old photo of Nick, his dad and his brothers. It was back in its baggie.

"You can have this back now," Burrows said.

He looked into the drawer one more time but stopped. Nick thought he resembled a magician reaching into his bag of tricks.

"I don't know what to make of it, but maybe you will."

The cop pulled out an item that looked like a flat black Frisbee. It appeared to be made of thick cloth.

"Any idea why he would have this?"

Nick was dumbfounded. He turned the thing over in his hands. "I don't even know what it is," he said.

Burrows took it back and gently pushed his hand through the center of it. It expanded into its original shape.

It was a top hat.

CHAPTER TWENTY

Nick pulled the one and only suit he owned out of his bedroom closet. Luckily it was black. He was getting ready to leave for the cemetery and Nevin's burial. But first things first. He reached down and took his short story out from beneath his bed. He read the last entry he'd made: *And wonder if he's even Peter anymore at all.*

He remembered thinking that, although he was not sure exactly how the story would go, things would end badly for Pete. In fact, he expected Peter to be dead at the story's conclusion.

But now, as he looked at it again, he wasn't so sure.

"This might be your lucky day, Pete," he said to himself.

If he's even Peter anymore at all.

There might be a better way to end the story, but at that moment he couldn't think of one. He grabbed a thick black marker off his desk and beneath the last line wrote two words:

THE END

Snow in Pittsburgh was rare in early November, but the narrow gravel path that ran through some pine trees separating the parking area from the cemetery was covered in a light dusting.

Nick thought that a cold blustery day was appropriate for the occasion.

He had picked Gina up on the way. Other than the two of them and the pastor, there were few visitors at the gravesite. As they walked, Nick spotted both Dean and Mark DeFazio and officer Burrows. Gina's mom was there too.

His own mother was not. She was still in the hospital but would be released later that day. He suggested delaying the burial until she could attend, but she dismissed it.

"You go take care of your brother," she said in the hospital the night before.

"So how did he get that hat?" Gina asked as they walked. She was wearing a short black dress and high heels. She hung onto his arm so she wouldn't slip in the snow.

"God only knows," he said. "I asked my mom but she didn't even know what I was talking about. She said it must have been was a Sampson thing." "And it was just sitting there in the nest?" She looked over and he nodded.

"Please stop calling it that," he chided her.

"You been back?"

"No." He didn't say it, but he would never step foot in that little clearing again. He couldn't. In some ways, it was as much Nevin's final resting place as the cemetery he was standing in.

"I've been meaning to ask you about your nightmares too," Gina said. "Still going on?"

"A little, but it's better," he said. "Fingers crossed." He looked over and she smiled. *A man could get lost in that smile,* he thought.

They arrived at the grave site, and Nick was surprised to see the casket had already been lowered. It had been a while since he attended a burial, but he thought that final act took place after the prayers had been said.

Gina pointed to the headstone.

"That's nice, "she said. He didn't tell her that Mr. DeFazio had paid for it and would not settle for the smaller stone that Nick suggested. Only the best, the old man said. "Where did that verse come from? A song?"

Nick told her that he actually wrote the epitaph himself. He left out the fact that he had basically just reworked a stanza from a poem he remembered from high school.

The epitaph read:

A small sad lad doth sweetly say,

In absence oft I do regret thee;

And though you may wander far away, Never once will I forget thee.

The pastor called the small group together and read a few Bible passages. He sang a shortened version of Amazing Grace (and had a surprisingly nice voice, Nick thought) and then said a final prayer.

"Amen," the group said in unison.

The few visitors then walked over and expressed their condolences to Nick. Gina's mom was the last to leave.

When they were alone, Gina asked Nick if he was ready to go, but he said he wanted to take one last look at the grave.

He walked over and stared down at the beautiful walnut casket that would soon be covered with six feet of Western Pennsylvania dirt. He bent down and scooped up a handful of the freshly-turned earth and let it sift through his fingers.

"See ya soon, Nevin," he said. "Rest easy big brother."

He took the photo of the Sampson men from his breast pocket, brought it to his lips and kissed it. Then he dropped it into the grave.

Nick was ready to walk over to Gina when his eyes caught on something else sitting on top of the casket. He thought he had to be imagining it. *Stress is getting to you old boy. That is not what you think it is.*

He motioned Gina over and pointed down into the hole. At first, she thought he was pointing at the photo, but then she spotted the other item. The stunned look on her face told Nick that he was not imagining it.

Resting on the casket next to the photo was a rose petal. It was blood red.

o o o

As Gina and Nick approached the empty parking lot, a pickup truck drove by on the road outside the cemetery. The radio blared, and even with the windows rolled up against the cold, Nick recognized the tune immediately. It was the same Fleetwood Mac song he heard in Pocataw after Michelle walked out of his life that summer.

"If I could, baby, I'd give you my world. Open up, everything's waiting for you," Nick sang softly.

"What?" Gina asked.

He pointed to the truck as it drove off. "The song," he said.

"Oh right." She stopped.

"It's a breakup song, Nick," she said "You know that, right?"

He smiled. "Is it?"

As Gina watched, Nick loosened his tie and undid the top button of his dress shirt. He took off the necklace with the seagull pendant and held it out for a second so she could see it. Then he put it around Gina's neck.

He reached down and took her hand in his.

They walked on down the path.

THE END

o o o

Made in United States
North Haven, CT
29 July 2023

39695058R00152